"What Are You Doing In My Bed?"

Panic flattened Leigh to the mattress. "You sleep here?"

"Sometimes," the man's deep voice rumbled.

Dressed only in her bra and panties, Leigh hitched the black satin sheet over her bare shoulder.

"You really should have taken everything off," he whispered. "To better enjoy the sheets. They're the finest quality."

"I am here on business. I didn't mean to fall asleep. I was locked in here and thought I'd take advantage of the—"

"You are in my bed. We have slept together."

Leigh swallowed tightly. "You sound as if…you know, we've been intimate—and that isn't true."

He shifted slightly and something she didn't understand slammed against her, taking her breath away. The massive bed seemed to slant, nudging her toward him on an erotic wave of satin sheets.…

HEARTBREAKERS

He'll stir his woman's senses, and when she's dizzy with passion…he'll propose!

Dear Reader,

Welcome to Silhouette Desire, where you can spice up your April with six passionate, powerful and provocative romances!

Beloved author Diana Palmer delivers a great read with *A Man of Means,* the latest in her LONG, TALL TEXANS miniseries, as a saucy cook tames a hot-tempered cowboy with her biscuits. Then, enjoy reading how one woman's orderly life is turned upside down when she is wooed by *Mr. Temptation,* April's MAN OF THE MONTH and the first title in Cait London's hot new HEARTBREAKERS miniseries.

Reader favorite Maureen Child proves a naval hero is no match for a determined single mom in *The SEAL's Surrender,* the latest DYNASTIES: THE CONNELLYS title. And a reluctant widow gets a second chance at love in *Her Texan Tycoon* by Jan Hudson.

The drama continues in the TEXAS CATTLEMAN'S CLUB: THE LAST BACHELOR continuity series with *Tall, Dark...and Framed?* by Cathleen Galitz, when an attractive defense attorney falls head over heels for her client— a devastatingly handsome tycoon with a secret. And discover what a ranch foreman, a virgin and her protective brothers have in common in *One Wedding Night...* by Shirley Rogers.

Celebrate the season by pampering yourself with all six of these exciting new love stories.

Enjoy!

Joan Marlow Golan

Joan Marlow Golan
Senior Editor, Silhouette Desire

Please address questions and book requests to:
Silhouette Reader Service
U.S.: 3010 Walden Ave., P.O. Box 1325, Buffalo, NY 14269
Canadian: P.O. Box 609, Fort Erie, Ont. L2A 5X3

Mr. Temptation
CAIT LONDON

Silhouette® Desire®

Published by Silhouette Books

America's Publisher of Contemporary Romance

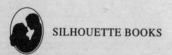 SILHOUETTE BOOKS

ISBN 0-373-76430-8

MR. TEMPTATION

This edition published by arrangement with Harlequin Books S.A.

® and TM are trademarks of Harlequin Books S.A., used under license. Trademarks indicated with ® are registered in the United States Patent and Trademark Office, the Canadian Trade Marks Office and in other countries.

Visit Silhouette at www.eHarlequin.com

Printed in U.S.A.

CAIT LONDON

is an avid reader and an artist who plays with computers and maintains her Web site, http://caitlondon.com. Her books reflect her many interests, including herbs, driving cross-country and photography. A national bestselling and award-winning author of category romance and romantic suspense, Cait has also written historical romances under another pseudonym. Three is her lucky number; she has three daughters, and her life events have been in threes. Cait says, "One of the best perks about this hard work is the thrilling reader response."

To the men, women and children who lost their lives
in the September 11, 2001, New York City and
Washington, D.C., tragedies, and to their families.

One

Jarek Stepanov braced himself against the Pacific tide, careless of the chilling water rising to his thighs. The seaweed moved, almost caressingly, around his legs, the predawn fog enveloping him in the scent of saltwater and memories.

Like a lover flirting for his attention, guilt whispered to him as the shore's sand slid beneath his boots.

But then he had no lover, nor the young wife he still loved and mourned, did he?

A mile northward from southern Washington State's shores, Deadman's Rock loomed. Concealed by the fog, it jutted from the tide to mock him. Had it killed Annabelle? Had a sudden fierce swell sent her small boat crashing against the black rock with enough force to topple her overboard? Jarek reached down to crush the seaweed in his fist, to hurl it out onto the black swells of water. How much of it had twined around his young wife, thwarting her struggles to rise to the surface? She'd looked so pale and small, floating in that bed of seaweed, washing slowly to shore.

The tide had been up then, separating the fingerlike peninsula from the mainland of southwest Washington State. A roundabout road could take one from the small town of Amoteh to the beautiful lush grass peninsula called Strawberry Hill. Yet the quickest way to reach it was through the passage between Deadman's Rock and the shore. The sweet name the hill bore belied the dark curse that had taken lives.

Jarek scrubbed his rough, workman's hands over his face and they came away shaking and damp with tears that he'd let no one see. He should have taken his wife across to Strawberry Hill, easily accessible by a small motorboat. He should have…

But Annabelle hadn't wanted to wait until he'd finished that rocking chair for a high-paying customer, just as she hadn't wanted to wait for another try at the baby she wanted—they both wanted. "I don't care if the doctor said to wait," she'd said. "Two miscarriages are enough and now *I want a baby*. The time is right for me to conceive—right now. I feel it. Let's go to Strawberry Hill—"

That last wild argument echoed in him now to the sound of the waves, and the chilling vision of Annabelle's empty boat floating back to shore shot straight to his heart once more. Still attached to the boat, the outboard motor had been lifted out of the water.

No one knew the whys and hows of her death because the day was bright and serene in the sun. Yet he had been called when Annabelle's body came floating amid the seaweed, a few scarlet wild strawberries mixed with the greenish-black leaves.

The lights of the small coastal town, Amoteh, where Jarek had grown up, were dim in the distance. The offshore buoy clanged in the fading morning fog, a few seagulls rising above the water. Just returning from a long hauling trip to the Midwest, Jarek inhaled the salt air and let the feeling of home wrap around him.

He should have taken his wife that day.

Jarek glanced at the pines rising in the distance, across that small deadly inlet which caught the dim, mid-May light in a gleaming silver streak now. The jutting black rock which cut into the sky to mark the passage had joined with the ocean's force to crush more than one ancient seafarer's ship. The light marking it now swept the fog eerily.

Perhaps Deadman's Rock had taken Annabelle's life. And perhaps it was true, too, that the ancient Hawaiian chieftain's curse on Strawberry Hill was still powerful.

Jarek should have taken more time with Annabelle, and with his marriage. But he hadn't ten years ago, and now he had no part of Annabelle to hold, to love, only the memories and the guilt.

Jarek lifted his face to the morning enveloping him, listened to the pounding of his empty heart and tried to will his wife back to him on the black waves. *Annabelle...Annabelle.* The name called to him, echoed in the sound of the waves as the first seagull gleamed ghostly pale in the dawn.

Showered and changed into jeans, Jarek tipped his chair back and propped his bare feet on his porch railing. Overlooking the Pacific Ocean, his one-room home was weathered and small and neat, unlike the modern home he'd built for his bride. He'd packed everything of sentimental value into a shadowy room at his father's furniture shop. He'd covered it with a tarp, but the restless memories of Annabelle couldn't be packed away—how badly she'd wanted a baby after two miscarriages. A family lived in their house now, with children's swings in the backyard and diapers hung on the clothesline.

Jarek pushed away the soft pain that came when he thought of the dreams he had shared with Annabelle. The tide was rising slowly now, just two hours after his return from the buying trip. Out on the finger jetty, a few odd fishermen were making themselves comfortable, settling in for the morning, bait buckets at their sides. Small, familiar fishing boats rode the waves nearby, and the men called friendly taunts to each other. In the distance, boats bobbed, moored to a pier, while another big pier lined with tourist shops thrust into the water.

The wind and water and sand of Amoteh were home, filling Jarek after his two-week buying and hauling trip to Missouri and Arkansas.

Jarek held a leftover rolled pancake in one hand and a mug of coffee in the other. He watched the bright sun skim the ocean swells, the seagulls soar against the clear blue sky, and let peace flow over him—as much peace as a man who had lost part of his heart could find.

Few people knew how deeply he grieved, the guilt that plagued him for not going with Annabelle that day as she'd asked. But one look from his brother and parents, and he knew they understood.

His favorite blueberry pancakes had been waiting at his mother's breakfast table. Mary Jo Stepanov's blond Texas beauty had glowed as she saw her son; Jarek's Russian father, Fadey, had hugged him soundly, kissed both his cheeks in the old-world greeting, then hurried outside to croon over the heavy seasoned walnut and oak planks that Jarek had hauled from Missouri and Arkansas.

Bright and cheerful, his mother's kitchen was rich with the custom oak cabinets Fadey Stepanov had made for his wife. The rest of the house was spacious, huge uncluttered windows overlooking the smooth, sandy Pacific shore where as children Jarek and his older brother, Mikhail, had run and fished and dug razor clams. Offshore, they would trap Dungeness crabs in season and sell them to the shops on the tourists' pier, or they'd fish for "bottom fish"—sea bass, rock and ling cod. And they helped their father at Stepanov's Furniture.

In lazy summer days, they would lie in the lush grass of Strawberry Hill and talk of lifting the curse Chief Kamakani had long ago placed on the land—it would only take a woman who knew her own heart to dance gracefully before his grave. They dreamed of how furious the chief must have been, stolen from his homeland and enslaved by whalers, and how he might have raged and cursed the land in which he died.

Maybe it was Jarek's passionate Russian blood, but the curse had always been ominous, more real after Annabelle's curious death.

A distance away from the tourist pier that provided Amoteh with seasonal income stood the Stepanov home. The jutting wood and rock structure with sprawling porches overlooked the ocean, Fadey Stepanov's statement that a poor Russian immigrant could build a lasting future. Inside, Mary Jo's Texas influence softened the massive wood furniture her husband created with soft mauve cotton throws, landscape paintings of sprawling fields and cattle. An ornate Russian *samovar,* a combination teapot and tea-brewing device, stood on a silver tray, surrounded by glasses with metal holders. In the kitchen, a string of chili peppers hung scarlet against the wood panels, brown glazed Mexican pots lining one shelf.

Clean lines of Stepanov furniture filled every room, demonstrating Fadey's love for his family and home. As a passionate immigrant with nothing but his pride, a loving heart and strong body, he'd claimed the wealthy Texas beauty. In return, Mary Jo had given Fadey her love and two sons who bore her green eyes and his dark brown waving hair.

Townspeople said that Jarek had gotten his passion for life from Fadey's Russian blood, while Mikhail laid claim to Mary Jo's more elegant, controlled nature. Or was it that Mikhail concealed his emotions better? Or more wisely?

As a top manager in the Mignon International Resort chain, Mikhail had set a course to bring more income to Amoteh. As a result of his success, he had lost his socialite wife.

On the hill above the sleepy, small town, the sprawling, luxurious Amoteh Resort boldly thrust its modern wood sections at the sky, windows flashing in the sun. There, tourists could swim in the massive indoor or outdoor pools, play tennis or golf, hike the pine-studded trails or walk down to the shore.

They could have massages and attend business retreats, and Amoteh residents had employment.

In contrast to his older brother, Jarek was what he was—a plain man who enjoyed nature, good wood beneath his hands, and life's small pleasures. In a few minutes, he would go down to the shop, help unload the heavy, rough planks he'd hauled from the Midwest. He'd enjoy his father crooning lovingly again over the properly seasoned wood.

As Jarek sat on his porch, telephone messages played from within the house, a woman's voice purring over the lines. Jarek frowned; he'd delighted in Marcella's company at last summer's Amoteh's Saturday night mixer, an invitation from Mikhail to "even up all the single women." Jarek had enjoyed the dance and the women and perhaps he had gotten a little drunk, but finding Marcella in his bed later had ended the pleasure. At thirty-six, he felt only one woman belonged in his bed, the woman who had held his heart…and she was gone.

Ten years ago he should have taken time to go with Annabelle, but she had made the trip before—the weather was good, but she was angry with him. He ran through that day again, sorting through why nothing should have happened to Annabelle. But it did, and he wasn't with her.

He listened as Linda Baker's message invited him to supper and slyly noted that her daughter had just gotten divorced. As children, Deidre and Jarek had dug razor clams together and she'd told him her dreams of her would-be prince that she had now just divorced after three children.

Jarek shredded the remainder of the pancake, hurling the pieces a distance from his house. The seagulls, ravenous in the morning, swooped to feed, pristine white against the brown sand, beach grass swaying as they flew and settled. Sandpipers hurried for their share.

In just two weeks, June's summer tourists would begin sailing and fishing and skimming the main pier's shops. Chartered boats would be filled, and unfamiliar boats would unfurl their sails to the wind.

The town named Amoteh, meaning strawberries in the Native American Chinook language, would come to life, catering to the tourists. The visitors to Mikhail's Amoteh Resort would stay in luxurious rooms furnished with Stepanov furniture. That experience often led to custom-made orders, enough for Stepanov Furniture to hire a few men during the slow tourism season and some after-school students.

Jarek sipped his coffee and enjoyed the slight breeze winnowing through his hair, flowing over his bare chest. After the Amoteh Resort was deserted that night—except for a few off-season guests—he'd haul the new Stepanov bookcase model into the showroom, dust and clean a bit, and settle down to enjoy the night and the ocean and his homecoming.

He inhaled the salt air and studied the sandpipers racing up and down shoreline, sometimes hidden by a pile of driftwood.

It was good to be back home.

In the Stepanov Furniture display room, Leigh Van Dolph tried to refuse the invitation of the sprawling walnut bed and couldn't. She had to rest, even for a moment, so she sat on the bed. She kicked off her heels and tossed her heavy briefcase onto the bed and unbuttoned her suit jacket.

She studied the run in her panty hose. It represented a futile day trying to catch the manager of the luxurious Amoteh Resort.

One look at her wristwatch told her that at six o'clock in the evening, Mikhail was probably dining. Clients were always more receptive after a meal, and she studied the furniture showroom that she had wandered into as she waited to catch him. The clean style of the walnut bed was heavily made, the wood smoothed to perfection, and matched the other pieces. The promotion advertisement on the dresser had said that the Stepanov furniture was sturdy and made to last.

"Get Mikhail Stepanov to agree to a Bella Sportswear shop

in his resort and we can get every luxury resort in the world to do the same thing. The Amoteh is his baby, a mark of how much the Mignon Resort chain trusts him. It's remote with little to offer just now, but with Mikhail stirring business, it will. He's a tough cookie, Leigh, but well respected and a trend setter. He's out to build that resort, and we want to get in on the bottom floor. Get him to sign a contract with us, and you'll get a bonus for that and every resort that lets us in,'' Morris Reed, Leigh's boss and friend had promised.

Leigh groaned softly. Her parents' latest escapade had cost her a hard-won appointment with Stepanov. Concerned for them, she hadn't called to reschedule the appointment. Wrapped in her parents' legal and medical dramas, she'd desperately tried to call Stepanov. At the time, the Amoteh was experiencing a redo of their phone system and the lines were dead at those brief moments when she could call. Then after a frantic day, another disaster: Ed's negative reaction to the medication had terrorized her and as a result of critical overload, she had simply missed the appointment.

She loved her family desperately, putting them first in all instances. Still wrapped in sixties' flower-power, Ed and Bliss were more her children, than she was theirs. Their latest sit-in, protesting the demolition of a famous but unsalvageable seaman's hotel, had cost Leigh time and a hefty check. Then Ed, as he preferred to be called, had appendicitis. Untethered by the realities of life that Leigh had faced for them since she was a child, they'd let their insurance lapse. She'd had to borrow money for an attorney and for paying Ed's medical bills in cash.

She needed the bonuses Morris offered just to keep her family safe; she was willing to humble herself before Stepanov to get the Amoteh Resort contract.

Leigh groaned again and ran a hand over the soft aqua-and-mauve striped bedspread; she wished she could curl beneath it and sleep.

But she couldn't. She had to catch the elusive manager of

the Amoteh, and snare him into agreeing to place a Bella Sportswear shop in his resort. The original appointment with Mikhail Stepanov had been for two weeks ago—before she'd had to deal with her parents' sit-in, jailing and her father's appendicitis attack.

She couldn't explain her family's instability to Stepanov, a man she wanted to influence in business. His secretary had tossed her invented excuse back at her with a stark note: "Mr. Stepanov has little patience for people who make appointments and do not keep them."

In the Stepanov showroom, Leigh yawned and stretched, feeling the economy rental car's miles and Seattle's traffic in every muscle. Her flight from San Francisco had been late, placing her into the city's morning rush hour traffic. A stress-filled three-hour drive had taken her to Amoteh, and she'd spent the rest of the day lurking in the huge resort, trying to corner the manager.

She'd seen Stepanov in the hallway—a tall, cold-looking man—and the run in her stocking resulted from a confrontation with a barbaric-looking plant stand as she had hurried after him—an unsuccessful effort.

Wearily Leigh pulled her cellular phone from her briefcase and dialed her parents' number.

"Ed is just fine, Precious," Bliss stated happily at the other end of the line.

Leigh shook her head at her birth name, Precious Blossom, which she had legally changed when she was twenty-one. She was now thirty-four, a Bella sales representative driven to succeed, and managing not only her life, but that of her parents and one very immature adult brother. "You'll stay then, won't you, Bliss? I mean—Ed needs rest."

She loved them more than her pride and her own life. She wanted only the best for her family and nothing could happen to them. She had to keep them safe and well.

"We moved out of the hotel that you liked, Precious. Ed wanted home—the van—and the hotel people didn't like me tie-dying T-shirts in the bathroom tub. They were so rude and picky. You know, all that anger the manager displayed isn't good for his spiritual alignment.''

Leigh inhaled slowly and took down the manager's number at the campground in which her parents were staying—after being evicted from a grocery store parking lot. The van's brightly colored flower decor and rust weren't wanted near better establishments. "Please, Bliss. I know it's important for Ed's karma to be in tune with the universe, but the campground sounds nice. Right now, it's really important that you don't lose the mobile telephone I gave you, okay? I'm trying very hard to push a deal through that means a hefty bonus, and I need your support.''

"Well, of course, Precious. You've always had our support and our love. But you need to relax. You're too geared to physical things, like money. You need to explore your inner self, listen to the voices within you, and develop your soul power. You have a tremendous soul, dear. Your capacity for love is unlimited. Stop worrying about your accounts and tapping your calculator, sweetheart. Go with the flow.''

After talking with Ed and extracting a somewhat whimsical promise that her parents wouldn't answer the "call of the universe winds" and leave the campground for parts unknown, Leigh settled down on the showroom bed. At her frantic life pace, balancing work and her family, she was used to catching rest when she could.

She nestled her head on the soft pillow. Outside the Stepanov showroom, the resort seemed to be quieting from the pre-busy season bustle. Leigh glanced at her watch. She'd arrived at two o'clock in the afternoon to find the Amoteh's staff working furiously trying to prepare for the heavy tourist season. After hours of hunting the elusive manager, she realized it was now almost six o'clock, and she had only napped since bailing her parents out of jail two weeks ago and worrying about Ed's appendicitis attack.

All she needed was one Bella shop in the very discriminat-

ing Amoteh Resort, just a finger hold on a massive, respected chain. All Leigh had to do was to catch Stepanov, a reportedly "tough sell" and pin him to a contract.

But Mikhail Stepanov was not available to anyone missing an appointment—with Stepanov, there were no second chances. His stern, gray-haired secretary had made that very clear, her rangy, tall body blocking the doorway to his office. "Mr. Stepanov said to leave your card. He is on a conference call now and cannot be disturbed. You realize that the Amoteh is part of Mignon International's worldwide chain and any ideas for shops are usually settled by the main office in Seattle—why don't you try there? Here's the address. I'm certain that if your sportswear company has a good reputation, they might talk with you."

"'Here's the address,'" Leigh repeated drowsily, as she snuggled into the inviting showroom bed in the Stepanov Furniture showroom. She had no doubt that her business card and request to see the manager had long ago been pitched into the trash.

A cart rolled by outside the showroom, but Leigh was too tired to rise. She'd rest a bit, and when the resort was peaceful, she'd catch Stepanov.

She awoke hours later to find the resort quiet, the moonlight reflecting the swimming pool's water upon the showroom's ceiling. The showroom door had been locked from the outside.

Leigh yawned and tried the door, calling out lightly, because if she were caught, she would try to be indignant. Stepanov might be more accommodating then, because his hotel staff had been inefficient. She yawned again and shook her head. She wasn't upset. She was warm and dry and in a soothing room with a luxurious bed. It was more than she had had in days.

After Ed and Bliss's latest confrontation with the police and Ed's operation, this delay was trivial. Stepanov wasn't leaving his resort just before the first wave of tourists. He'd be there first thing in the morning and she'd be waiting for him. And she was very, very good.

She stripped off her suit jacket and ruined hose. It seemed only logical to take advantage of a good bed and a peaceful evening. Leigh removed her blouse and slacks, hanging them carefully in the beautiful walnut armoire. With a yawn, she slid beneath the cool, inviting black satin sheets and listened to the surf's rhythms. She'd be up early, and when the door was unlocked in the morning, she'd wait until she could leave, unseen.

Clad only in her practical white bra and panties, Leigh stirred in the black satin sheets, far more erotic and sensual and expensive than the cotton ones she had at her apartment—when she could manage to sleep there.

All she had to do was be fresh and bright in the morning and convince Stepanov to place a Bella Sportswear shop in the Amoteh.

Ed and Bliss and Winter Child, alias her brother who had renamed himself Ryan, all depended on her. She had to provide for them.

She had to get Stepanov to agree to a Bella Sportswear shop. She had to get the lucrative bonus her boss had promised her. She had to… She had to…

Leigh stirred and managed to rouse, lifting her arm to study her wristwatch. At three o'clock in the morning, she estimated a good three more hours before the Amoteh's household and maintenance crews started to arrive.

The reflection of the pool's water danced across the ceiling, and she could just barely hear the sound of the ocean—and someone else's slow, deep breathing.

The door had been locked—she turned her head slightly on the pillow to the man who lay sprawled beside her, sleeping on top of the luxurious quilt. His hair was longer than her curly short cut, his deep waves spreading across the black satin pillow.

Shadows hid his eyes and stubble covered his jaw. Moonlight gleamed on the planes of his brow and cheek, and flowed over the body of a powerful man much taller than she. He lay with his flannel shirt open, one big hand resting peacefully upon his chest and the other—

Leigh slowly looked down to the warm, broad weight on her thigh—his other hand lay possessively on her thigh. His fingers widened and flexed and smoothed as she watched, her heart pounding. Lying, clad in his worn flannel shirt, worn jeans and his socks, he smelled of soap, lemon, wood and the tang of salty sea air and of man—that dark, mysterious essence curled around her.

"What are you doing in my bed?" the man's deep voice rumbled sleepily as his weight shifted, and he turned to fully face her.

Panic flattened Leigh to the bed. "Your bed? You mean you sleep here?"

"Sometimes." His voice was deep and rolling with that slight accent, almost musical.

Leigh hitched the black satin sheet over her bare shoulder, and tried to calm herself. With the dark heavy wood and black satin as a background, the man looked sexy and terrifying as he smiled slowly, that seemingly drowsy gaze taking in her face and inch by inch following her throat down to the crevice of her breasts. Leigh jerked the sheet to her chin.

"You really should have taken off everything," he whispered unevenly, and a wisp of something tingled along her body, lifting the hairs on her nape. She sensed that he wasn't sleepy now at all, rather he was very alert and focused on her as he added, "To better enjoy the sheets. They're the finest quality."

"Would you mind leaving, please?" Leigh asked shakily as the man smoothed her hair with that big, hard hand. His palm brushed her cheek lightly and the calluses on it said he worked with his hands. No doubt he had tried the quality of the sheets with a lover.

Something undefinable was humming in the air between them. And it wasn't coming from her. "What are you doing here?"

He shrugged and one finger strolled down her cheek. "You're very warm—I'd guess you're blushing. That leads me to believe that you might not be waiting for your lover, for a tryst in a furniture showroom."

Leigh blinked; she was too locked in her own struggles to care much about passion. With too many responsibilities placed on her at an early age, her passions ran to security, her parents in one place and money in her bank account.

She sensed that this man would know about passion—how to stir it, how to savor it. His intimate study of her sent a wave of odd sensations through her. The bed beneath her seemed to slant and shift and the sheets slid erotically over her skin. "People do that?"

He shrugged again and she shivered as his mouth curved slightly in a sleepy, sensuous smile. "I find them once in a while when I come to tidy up."

"You unlocked the door. You must be a maintenance man or a night watchman. Please go. I'll get dressed and—"

"But why are you here?" he asked in that deep, husky voice, and the moonlight caught the glint of his eyes beneath those long eyelashes, and again his gaze slowly moved down her body, covered the quilt.

Leigh hadn't had time for dating, and certainly not sex, and the man's look had unsettled her. He was definitely interested and on the prowl. She was all alone, her phone stashed in her briefcase, and from the look of those broad shoulders and that tall, fit body, he could easily overpower her. "I've had self-defense classes. I could hurt you," she bluffed shakily.

That lifted brow said he was amused. "Why are you here?" he repeated, and then added in a lower, huskier tone, "In my bed."

"I needed sleep—"

"This is a resort. Though it's not fully opened for summer,

there are a few rooms reserved for off-season guests who don't mind the rain. The rates are discounted now.''

"I read their brochure, and the rates are still very expensive. I couldn't afford a room here right now and I wasn't going to stay. I was just going to do business with Mr. Stepanov and then leave. You know Mr. Mikhail Stepanov, don't you? I wouldn't want to upset him by telling him that you were bothersome.''

"Me? Bothersome? You are in *my* bed. We have slept together.'' The statement was almost arrogant, his voice carrying just a whisper of an accent.

Leigh swallowed tightly. If he wanted to disconcert her, he knew exactly how to do it. "You sound as if—you know, we've been intimate—and that isn't true.''

He shifted slightly, gracefully, only just that turn of his head, but waves of something she didn't understand slammed against her, taking her breath away. And that massive bed seemed to slant again, nudging her toward him on an erotic wave of satin sheets. Of course, the bed wasn't moving—it was sturdy and the mattress good—but the sensations within her made it seem as if it were drawing her to him on a sensual wave.

She tried for logic; she wasn't a sensual woman and whatever she was experiencing now just wasn't reality. "I am here on business. I didn't mean to fall asleep, but I did. I was locked in here and thought I'd take advantage of the—''

Those deep-set eyes glittered, taking in her hair, her face, her throat. "Do you often fall asleep in strange places?''

"I needed the rest. I've been on the move for two weeks and I'm exhausted. Yes, I do fall asleep where and when I can. I haven't had a regular night's sleep for ages. Now, if you don't mind.''

"I'm tired, too.'' The man rolled over, his broad back to her. "Go to sleep. You're quite safe here.''

"Leave.''

"No, you leave.''

"I was here first," Leigh stated automatically. She'd learned early in childhood that she had to hold her own, keeping what was dear to her—and sleep and that bed were very dear right now.

He didn't answer, but lay between her and the armoire. Dressed only in her bra and panties, she didn't feel like exposing her body to the stranger. Leigh wished she were braver, but she wasn't. She had the sudden sense that the man was guarding her. No one had ever watched over her, not even as a child. She'd found security only in herself and her ability to survive. Her parents loved her, but they were not always alert to dangerous people.

She lay stiffly on the far side of the bed. *She was not giving up her badly needed rest because an oversize handyman had invaded the only bed she'd managed in days.*

"Who takes care of you?" he asked softly in the night, that accent lurking in his deep voice.

"I do. I take care of everyone," she answered sleepily. She'd shared enough odd situations in her lifetime, trying to catch sleep on a bus, in the subway, on an office couch, and other places. Accustomed to dealing with strangers doing the same thing, Leigh decided to take advantage of the hours left to sleep. "And if you bother me, or breathe a word of this to Mr. Stepanov, I'll find some way to have him fire you. This contract means everything to me, and I wouldn't hesitate to make your life living hell if you even come close to ruining my chances."

"Mmm. Tough lady." He didn't sound frightened, rather amused.

He was only a handyman. He wasn't likely to exchange confidences with the lordly Mr. Stepanov; it didn't matter what she told him, so she did as a release for the frustration that had plagued her life. "If you think it's easy growing up in a van, taking care of parents who love you but who are totally irresponsible for their lives, you're mistaken. I've handled life and problems ever since I can remember. So you're not creating any more for me. I won't tell Mr. Stepanov that you probably sleep here every night, if you won't tell him that I— That I badly needed sleep and took advantage of this beautiful bed. You *know* he wouldn't like the hired help using his family's furniture display room. It would cost you your job. And I wouldn't hesitate to tell him. Got that?''

"Yes, dear," he answered sleepily. "Sleep well."

Leigh lifted her pillow and thrust it between them, punching it into a hard shape. The maintenance man probably slept here every night—either alone or with his lover. Leigh sniffed delicately and couldn't detect another woman's fragrance—all she caught was the scent of sea and lemon polish and man.

Two

Jarek held Leigh Van Dolph's business card to the rising dawn's light, which gently filled the showroom. As he considered the woman on the bed, his thumb skimmed the embossed logo of Bella Sportswear.

The hard prod of unexpected desire nettled him—if they were lovers, he would have taken her slowly, deeply as he awoke, aching. He hadn't thought desire would come to him again…his heart and hopes had come floating back to him, lifeless in a bed of seaweed. And yet, here was the stirring of his body, the quickening of his pulses as he caught the woman's light, provocative scent….

She had excited his senses, and he wasn't certain if he liked that surprise. Jarek breathed quietly, leaning back into the shadows, stunned by the physical need that had been dormant for years. He could almost taste that lush mouth, that smooth skin sliding beneath his lips. As long on the bottom as on the top, her lashes were the same shade as those short, spiraling curls—curls he longed to touch, to slide his finger through, letting them capture him in their silk. They gleamed richly—not pale as a blond, nor dark as raven, but somewhere between. A small, perfect ear escaped that curly cap, and Jarek's body tensed with the urge to cruise his lips over the shape, to tug at the small lobe with his teeth.

He ran his hand over his hair, shaken by the depth of his need, by his fascination with the woman who looked so small and sweet in the sprawling, heavily built bed.

The rest of her, pale and curved, was a man's pure erotic dream. She wasn't slender, but compact, her breasts full and cupped within the practical white bra. The black satin sheet slid across her waist and lower to tangle over one leg, then exposing one delicate foot. Her bare arm was flung across the black satin pillow as though it were her lover.

The lash of darkness and anger curled within him, an unfounded jealousy. *Did she have a lover?*

The question taunted him as she moved slightly and the soft flow of feminine flesh rippled and settled in the dim light.

Again the jolt of desire slammed into Jarek's body. Aching to touch her, to make love to her, he rubbed his hand briskly over the hard edge of a bureau.

He fought the hard thumping of his heart, the racking question of why this one woman? *Why, after all these years?*

Why, after an hour of wondering what to do with the woman on the bed, of fighting the feminine scent and the curves, had he settled down beside her to watch her breathe, to watch those brows draw together in a frown as some unpleasant worry strolled through her sleep?

Why had he wanted to spoon around her, place his hand on her breast and gather her close and rest as he hadn't for years?

Those eyes had widened with fear as she discovered him beside her. What color were they? Blue as the ocean? Black as the raven's wing? Green as emeralds? Gray as the churning dark clouds that preceded a stormy squall?

Jarek held his breath as she arched and stretched, the satin sheet kicked away. He wished he hadn't seen those jutting hipbones, the dip of her navel as she turned onto her stomach, her white cotton panties covering the soft roundness of her bottom.

His hand slashed across his mouth. The sight of her, warm, soft and feminine, tempted him to skim the flesh down her back, to slide his fingers beneath that cotton and—

The incredible tight heat of desire enclosed and shocked him. She'd be so warm, so—he inhaled the woman scent amid the others of lemon and wood, and his body stirred almost painfully, heavily, recognizing its need.

Jarek pushed from the shadows and quickly, quietly left the room, locking the door behind him. He leaned in the hallway shadows and breathed heavily, shaken by an awakening desire too harsh to ignore. He reached into a maid's cart left pushed against the wall and placed a Do Not Disturb sign on the showroom's heavy door. The sign wouldn't cause question; the staff understood that after working in the showroom, he sometimes stayed to enjoy it.

At six o'clock in the morning, the Amoteh Resort was like a great beast slumbering, waiting for the staff who would bustle down the halls, cleaning and readying for tourist season. A few off-season guests, taking advantage of discount prices, would make their way down to Amoteh, enjoying the shops there, and then the walks along the shoreline. Dressed in a perfectly tailored suit, Mikhail would soon course down the halls, clicking off fine points to the staff.

As he thought of his brother, Jarek passed the linen supply room and noted the maids' carts waiting to be filled. Mikhail was determined to make the three-year-old Amoteh Resort a success. It had been his dream and years in the planning; he wouldn't fail. Not only his well-deserved reputation as an intuitive businessman depended on the success of the new venture, but the livelihood of many employees residing in Amoteh. The insurance and benefits the Amoteh provided were the best, and it was due to Mikhail's insistence.

But his success had cost Mikhail a wife. She had wanted

New York and Broadway and plays and Acapulco and Cannes—she didn't want to spend her life ''wasting in a smelly little town.'' Mikhail had taken the surprise of divorce—and her abortion of his baby—silently, but his family understood. Stepanovs took marriage and children very seriously. Mikhail did not take failure well, and he wasn't likely to remarry. He devoted himself to building the Amoteh into a world-class resort; now business was his love, his game, his life.

In business, Mikhail was formidable. And Ms. Leigh Van Dolph wanted a contract from Mikhail; she was just as determined. Jarek smiled slightly; it would be interesting to see whose determination won, his cool brother's or Leigh's. She was a fighter who didn't give up easily; he'd seen that last night, expecting her to leave the bed. But she hadn't, and now she was desperate—because she loved her family.

Jarek understood family and love. In her position, he would be equally determined.

According to his parents, Mikhail had recently stormed about an irresponsible saleswoman who hadn't shown up for an appointment. He had no time to waste on poor businesspeople, and her delayed excuses didn't hold up. If the woman was that salesperson, she had little chance of swaying Mikhail, or even seeing him.

Jarek flicked the plain business card of Ms. Leigh Van Dolph, Senior Sales Rep of Bella Sportswear, against the stubble on his cheek. She'd been exhausted enough to take the first opportunity for sleep; she wasn't used to a man in her bed—the widening of her eyes and the stiffening of her body, the way she drew the satin sheet up to her chin told him that.

The erotic beckoning of the image slid by him again, stirring, taunting.

He tried to push it aside to think clearly. She'd grown up in a van and now she was a top salesperson wearing a suit and trying to impress Mikhail, a pretty hefty task.

Jarek stared out at the rising ocean tide beyond the howling winds. The day would bring rain and something else—he had to know why she stirred him so, why every beat of his heart told him to make love to her.

He smiled as he noted Mikhail, already dressed in a black suit and cruising the wide luxurious hallways like some dark knight sweeping through his castle. It was time to call in a brotherly favor.

Moments later, Mikhail sat at his desk and tapped an expensive pen on a yellow paper pad. The spacious wood-paneled office seemed to hum with Mikhail's energy, every piece of furniture chosen from Stepanov designs. The brothers were equally tall at six feet three inches and powerfully built; but Mikhail's dark brown hair was neatly clipped in contrast to Jarek's shoulder-length waves, a perfect demonstration of how different the brothers were—but where the Stepanov passions ran almost savagely proud, and in balance with that joyful and compassionate, there they were alike, understanding each other, linked by blood.

Jarek adjusted his length to the comfortable chair in front of the sprawling walnut office desk and placed his boots on a stack of paper.

Mikhail frowned at the boots and then at his brother. With the ease of an older brother dealing with a younger one, he lifted Jarek's boots and shoved a magazine beneath them. "She broke an appointment, Jarek. I don't do business with irresponsible people. She never called, or tried to explain— until she wanted another appointment. I don't do business like that. I can't be available to everyone, on their time, and I won't be. You say that right now she's sleeping on a Stepanov bed in the showroom—I owe her nothing. She's lucky she's not tossed out of here now—and maybe into jail. I will not have people sleeping wherever they wish—especially vagrants."

"She's responsible for a family, Mikhail. This isn't for herself."

After a thoughtful moment, Mikhail's scowl slowly eased into an unexpected grin. "You're woman-hunting, aren't you?

For some reason, she's gotten to you. Now this should be interesting. You've run from enough women, but now this one interests you. Why?"

Jarek scowled back at Mikhail. He knew when Mikhail was set to tease him. "Don't enjoy yourself too much, older brother. I'm just asking you to meet her, that's all, tonight at Mom and Dad's."

Mikhail's quick mind jumped to the next question. "Does she know you're my brother?"

When Jarek shook his head, Mikhail's grin widened. "So the game is already being played, and you don't know whether you want to enter it or not."

Jarek stood and stretched. Despite his easy appearance, he didn't like Mikhail's too-accurate assessment of his emotions—this was the first morning in years that he'd awakened next to a woman, wanting to make love to her. He wasn't certain why Leigh fascinated him, but she did.

"Mind your own business," he said lightly and prayed that her delicate scent wouldn't haunt him; he hadn't liked that too-sudden jolt of sensuality, his body hardening before he knew what had hit him. He knew that her scent came not from shampoos or perfumes, but from her skin, from the essence of the feminine woman she was. And it beckoned to him....

Leigh sat on the showroom bed she had just made, dressed and wondering what to do next. She held her briefcase, which contained her ruined panty hose, and studied her bare legs and her practical black pumps. The door was locked again, and she'd tidied herself as best she could, though there was no way she could straighten her hair without spray. It had caught the ocean air yesterday and now curls spiraled around her head, most unbusinesslike.

And from what she had heard, in business, Mikhail Stepanov was cold as ice, slashing through pleasantries. She understood men like him, preferred him to those who might play games—like the maintenance man of last night.

Leigh glanced at her wristwatch, which read seven o'clock, and tried to straighten her hair by tugging at it. When released, the curls immediately sprung back into spirals. If no one opened the locked door before— The lock clicked and she stood, holding her briefcase in front of her, a smile pasted on her face. If it were Stepanov, she'd have to immediately start complaining about his inefficient staff who locked her in—

Instead, the tall, lean handyman studied her. "I thought you were taller," he said slowly. "You seemed taller. I wondered about your hair—it's the rich color of copper, lit by fire, and your eyes are the color of dark honey."

His were the color of grass, green and lush; his hair was too long, shaggy and waving and thick—the color of rich brown sable. It begged for a woman to smooth it, to run her fingers through it, fisting it…and his mouth—she looked away from those lips curving almost tenderly as he looked closely at her. Again that electric prickle circled her, raising the hair on her nape.

He reached to run a fingertip around her lobe and Leigh shivered, jolted by the touch. "Ah. You're wearing earrings. The pearl studs suit you. Small, neat, feminine."

"I'm not that small." In her pumps, she barely reached his shoulder, but she was used to presenting herself with impact that compensated for her less than willowy height. She smoothed her navy pin-striped suit which with flowing lines produced that tall willowy look she desired. Her practical pumps added another inch or two.

There was nothing shrimpish about her height. Five foot six inches wasn't under par. She wasn't tall and lithe, but she was serviceable—muscular enough to move her display luggage and suitcases and to run fast to catch airplanes when late for boarding.

She wouldn't let him intimidate her. She inhaled, bracing herself for another confrontation with him, and straightened, saying with as much dignity as she could manage, "I'd appreciate it very much if you didn't say anything to Stepanov. Just let me out of here.''

"I thought you might like to freshen up," he offered, slowly pushing a finger into her hair, toying with it. "It changes color when it catches the sun. There is gold in it and flames.''

"Leave my hair alone. I would very much appreciate a chance to freshen up—and privacy," she returned, disliking this morning's gritty and rumpled feeling. She'd had enough of "rumpled" from her childhood, living in a van and moving from place to place. While she caught sleep where she could, she always tried to take care of her clothing and appearance— and an orderly life when her parents and brother would allow her, was essential.

She slapped his hand away and watched the amusement light those grass-green eyes. He smelled of soap and his dark brown hair was just as untamed as before, the scent of sea air clinging to him. In her research of the Amoteh Resort, she'd discovered that Stepanov preferred to hire locals, and this man's tanned skin said he spent time outdoors, the lighter laugh lines around his eyes crinkling. Those big broad hands and the width of his shoulders said he was a physical man and spent little time behind a desk.

She understood "desk-men." They understood tit for tat in the business world, and spared little time for pleasantries that weren't getting them anything. She didn't understand the handyman's almost flirtatious interest in her. "I tip well for good service," she said to waylay any ideas that he might have of the payment form.

He'd shaved, the light gleaming on his cheeks and just that humorous turn of his lips, and she sensed that he was challenging her.

"Well, I do tip well," she repeated, just in case he was a bit dense. "I understand need and supply for good service.''

That curve of his mouth widened into a flashing grin. In that moment, he reminded her of a pirate—one who could easily capture a woman's heart.

She shook that image away, then resented the bobbing soft curls at her cheek. He might be entertained by the situation, but she wasn't. "Look. Just help me, and I'll make it worth your while, okay?"

He tilted his head, studying her face in that quiet, intent way that made her more uncertain than his power-packed grin. What was he thinking? That she would cry if Stepanov refused to see her? Well, she wouldn't because she was going to get that contract.

"Breakfast? The cook fixes mine sometimes. You'd have to eat with me, of course—or else the staff would show you the door. It's a big door with a hefty security lock. You wouldn't get in easily again."

Her stomach growled, mocking her, and there was no sense in approaching Stepanov with unseemly noises—let alone the light feeling in her head that came from skipping lunch and dinner yesterday. The granola bar she always carried in her briefcase was devoured long ago. "That would be very nice. I'd pay, of course."

Inwardly Leigh winced at the cost of meals at the expensive resort, but a contract with Stepanov was worth anything—even a meal with the man who was now studying her lips and disconcerting her.

"I really would appreciate a bathroom," she said unevenly and drew out the plastic bag from her briefcase, which contained her toothbrush and other toiletries.

He nodded briefly and leaned to peer outside, scanning the hallway. "Follow me. It wouldn't do for Mikhail—for Stepanov—to find you just yet. He is very big on first impressions for business people."

Leigh felt as though she were in an old spy movie as he took her hand, enclosing it with his big rough one, and pulled her quickly down the hallway to a suite. He opened the door and pulled her inside, nodding to the bathroom. "I'll stand watch. Don't be afraid. The door locks from the inside. Take your time. The cook won't be ready to serve my breakfast until after she's had her coffee and newspaper."

"Thank you. I'll be just a minute." Leigh rummaged in her briefcase, came up with her wallet and took two five-dollar bills from it. When he made no move to take the money she held out to him, she tucked it into his shirt pocket. She didn't like that tilt of his chin, that certain sense of pride and arrogance as those green eyes narrowed down at her. They weren't friendly now, but rather like cold, hard, cutting emeralds.

"You offend me," he stated baldly. "I want to help you, and you think money is my reason?"

"I appreciate your services," she said, trying for logic. She preferred to keep whatever passing relationship they had on a business basis. He was disturbing enough, without friendly intentions. "And you can probably use the money."

"Your thank-you was enough. I'll wait," he stated curtly.

Leigh reveled in the luxurious, steaming shower, feeling revitalized after shampooing her hair. She tried to blow dry the curls from it, but without her taming solution, the springy spirals returned. Mourning the loss of her demonstrator maillot suit, Leigh skimmed into the bikini she carried as a sales sample, stuffed her underwear into her briefcase and finished dressing.

Refreshed, feeling as if she could run Stepanov down and hog-tie him, she stepped from the bathroom and handed the damp towels to the man. He looked at them and then at her. "You've done this before."

"I've been in a few situations—yes. I dried the shower stall and took the soap and shampoo and cream with me. They'll just think that the room hasn't been serviced yet. Is there someplace you could dispose of those damp towels?"

Though he hadn't moved, she sensed a caress—his. Only his eyes had touched her. He spoke huskily, slowly. "In the kitchen. But first, I'd like to hear you say my name—Jarek. Say 'Jarek.'"

Leigh considered the request. It wasn't unreasonable, con-

sidering the gift of the luxurious shower. Perhaps she was too
uneasy, too sensitive because of her tension, the sale she had
to make. "Jarek."

"Again," he whispered, leaning down to her; his hand
braced against the wall at her head.

"Jarek." Why was she so breathless, her heart racing
wildly? All she could see were those green eyes, her face
caught in the dark centers. The sensations of rain on grass, the
wind moving through it caught her—an excitement she didn't
understand. She sensed changes and danger and mystery and
incredible awareness of who she was, who he was. Why?

He smiled briefly as if satisfied, nodded, and took her hand
again. He studied it within his larger one before saying briskly,
"Let's go to the kitchen. I'm starved."

A half hour later, Jarek and the hefty cook named Georgia
sat at the employees' long, pristine table in the massive stain-
less-steel kitchen. They watched Leigh devour her food, scraping her toast around the plate for the last bit.

She closed her eyes, savoring the taste, and sipped the fragrant house-blend coffee. Life would soon be good again, and
she would be in control once more. She would bag Stepanov,
tie up his account in a bow and serve him to Morris for her
bonus. "Thank you. That was delicious. How much do I owe
you?"

Georgia's cropped straight hair was covered by a practical
net that looked like a spiderweb as it crossed her forehead.
"Not a thing. I like a healthy appetite. I never quite saw a
woman dive into her food like that."

"I'm used to eating on the run—airport sandwiches, fast
food and whatever. But that was really, really good."

Leigh's impish grin startled Jarek. Her eyes were gold
honey now, startling in those long, burnished, dark lashes. He
could have looked at them all day—and night. Georgia
beamed and then looked at Jarek. "She's welcome in my
kitchen anytime. You're the first woman he's brought here,

you know. He lost his wife some time ago, and he's very particular. In fact, I don't know of one woman he's dated since—''

"We're not dating," Leigh stated firmly. "I really need to pay you. If Mr. Stepanov finds out that—"

Jarek placed the two five-dollar bills she'd given him on the table. "Buy something for Eldon, Georgia. How's his leg?"

"He doesn't like therapy. It hurts him, and that leg will never be the same, not after it got caught in the anchor's rope. Never the same."

Leigh's hand covered Georgia's hamlike, soft one. She foraged into her briefcase and placed a twenty on top of the fives. "Oh, I'm so sorry. Yes, please do buy him something special."

Georgia glanced at Jarek. "She's a feeling woman. Got a good heart."

He nodded slowly. "I think she needs to relax."

Who was he to input into her life? Did she ask for his suggestion? Leigh wondered darkly before turning her attention to the cook. "Thank you, Georgia. But I know how hard it is to manage sometimes. Just to survive takes everything. A little gift to make your husband feel better might do wonders."

Then Leigh remembered the tantalizing bonuses she needed to support her family. "Do you think Mr. Stepanov might have a slack time? I need to catch him. He avoided me yesterday. I'm afraid I didn't make a very good impression."

Georgia hesitated and frowned slightly as she glanced warily at Jarek; his lids were lowered, his expression impassive. "He is a very busy man," the cook said finally as she rose and left the table. "You come back."

Jarek leaned back to study Leigh. Then he said quietly, "I know where he has dinner. You might catch him there. He usually seems to be in a good mood."

"I really need to see him. Is there somewhere I can call you, if I can't get his attention today?" She disliked depending on this man. He seemed too confident, too arrogant, and he'd just given away the tip he'd deserved.

She resented that gesture. Her money and status were hard won. He'd acted very cavalier with money, and in her experience, those were usually the types who couldn't pay their bills.

Jarek's slow, appraising look unnerved Leigh, the air between them seeming to dance with tiny electric sparks. From how he had looked at her, touched her, she suspected he was a Romeo looking for new conquests. She didn't have time for games, or for tall, rugged sailor-types with sultry green eyes that took in everything about her, from her eyes and lips down to her throat and lower.

"I've got a house not far from here," he said. "I'll be there later. If you want, meet me and I'll take you to dinner where Stepanov eats sometimes."

With the experience of a woman who had engineered many such informal business meetings, Leigh asked, "Is it possible you could just introduce me and then leave? Do you know him that well?"

She didn't understand Jarek's grin. "I know him very well. We grew up together. He was not always wrapped up in business."

She would have Mikhail Stepanov in a friendly situation and she would get the account. And the bonus. "Oh, that's wonderful. A friend introducing me to Stepanov. I do appreciate it. That would be like a personal endorsement."

"Say Jarek," he said quietly, and an unfamiliar accent lurked in his deep voice. "I like it when you say my name."

Later, the ocean gleamed in the mist, the tide lapped at the sand near Jarek's beachfront home. The neat, gray-weathered small house didn't surprise her. One chair, equally weathered, sat on the porch overlooking the ocean. It said that the man's interests ran to something other than his home. Jarek probably didn't spend much time there; Leigh decided that he was probably too busy with come-ons.

The wind caught Leigh's curls, tossing them hopelessly as she limped toward the weathered house, the blister on her heel caused by the loss of her hose. She trudged through the damp sand, her pumps sinking into it, the strap of her briefcase cutting into her shoulder. Her suit was damp from the rain, her blouse clinging to her, and she felt as gloomy as the rainy day.

She resented having to come to Jarek, to have him help her. There was an arrogance to him that nettled, and she didn't have time to filter through all the uneasy sensations he could cause by just one look. With his looks, no doubt many other women had fallen beneath his spell, and Leigh didn't intend to be one of them.

Suddenly he was beside her, the wind pasting his light jacket and jeans against that powerful body, tugging at that long, wild hair. He looked as if he were a sailor, standing on the prow of a sailing ship long ago and as much a part of the scenery as the crashing waves. He placed his hands on his hips and grinned at her, taking in her sodden appearance, her wind-tossed curls. "Did you catch him?"

"He's elusive. He's avoiding me. You're not dressed for dinner."

"It's informal."

She frowned as she remembered hovering in the resort's luxurious halls, frantically using elevators up and down as she pursued the man who always seemed just a step ahead of her. One odd fact circled her—Stepanov knew she was in pursuit, he evidently wasn't happy with her for not making an appointment, and yet—yet he hadn't had her thrown out.

That gave her hope. Perhaps it was really true—that he just didn't have time with his busy schedule to talk with her.

Catching him at dinner, an easy conversation over good food, might create the perfect moment in which to make her pitch for Bella.

"You're that determined then—sinking so low as to ask a maintenance man to help you meet Stepanov?"

She shook her hair, careless of the curls bobbing at her

cheek. "Look. I'm too tired to play games. I've got a blister on my heel, I'm chilled to the bone, and my rental car died. If I get a cold, I can't meet Stepanov with sneezes and a runny nose. Also, when I get a cold, I'm not the most pleasant person in the world. I'm told that I actually snarl. I'll make it worth your while if this comes off. If it doesn't and you behave well, there's still something in it for you."

His rich laughter rolled over the ocean waves. "Well, let's go then."

"Fine," she said and didn't care that her tone was that of the doomed.

She gasped as Jarek picked her up easily, holding her close as she gripped her briefcase. She tried to make the leap from the businesswoman standing on the beach, to Jarek's easy handling of her.

"I'm just trying to save those shoes. The damp sand can make them come apart," he explained logically. "And there's that blister on your heel. Did you take care of it?"

"I was running after Stepanov all day. You think I had time to stop and pamper myself? He moves very fast and the Amoteh is huge with lots of hallways and closets and who knows what else. Anyway, he ducked me all day…. I can walk, you know. I'll take off my shoes."

"No," he answered firmly. "You will not. That blister could become infected."

She stared at him and gripped her briefcase closer. It seemed like an anchor in a world suddenly dominated by this big, powerful man. "Look, you—Jarek. I take care of myself and everyone else in my family. I've had enough of everything— the dead rental car, the nincompoop at the rental agency, Stepanov avoiding me, wearing a bikini as underclothes, the safety pin in my slacks where the button has come off, the arrogance of a man I barely know—but who, of course, is likely to remind me of how much I need him at any minute."

He continued walking toward the large, sprawling building a distance up the beach. In the light rain, the large square windows glowed and mixed with the scent of sea air and smoke. "Two things—one, you forgot to mention that we shared a bed last night, which was very significant to me. I haven't shared a bed with a woman for ten years, not since my wife."

She sniffed lightly at that, disbelieving that the man who had leaned so close and inhaled her fragrance and had looked so intently at her body would be without a woman for long. "Uh-huh. Sure. Of course. And the second thing?"

"You shouldn't ever tell a man that you're wearing a bikini beneath your clothes. It's more inviting than actually wearing it openly. Do you often model swimwear for your prospective clients?"

She didn't understand the fierce tone, nor the tightening of his arms, as if he wasn't letting anyone else have her, as if she were his. "I leave that to the long, leggy type. I am a professional you know—an important asset to Bella Sportswear and I try for a business appearance. I carry the sample suit to demonstrate the good fabric and how well our products hold up. It's handy in emergencies."

His arms relaxed slightly. "You realize that you are very curvaceous, and that the sight of you in skimpy clothing could excite men."

The thought was new to her. *She needed that contract.* "You think Stepanov might actually pay attention to me at say, a poolside meeting?"

"No. I do not." Jarek continued carrying her up the concrete steps to the wooden, jutting building.

"What's his favorite dinner topic?"

"Food."

She studied his set expression. "Why are you acting angry? You don't have to carry me, you know. And don't forget. I'll make it worth your while to leave just after we're introduced."

At the massive double wooden doors, Leigh said, "Put me down. You can't carry me into the restaurant—"

Just then the doors opened and Jarek carried her into a

sprawling, beautiful home. While she was still gaping, taking in the big solid furniture, the older man who looked like Jarek, with his arm around a tall, elegant woman, Jarek placed her in a large walnut chair and bent to slip off her shoes.

As Leigh gripped the smoothly finished arms of the chair and tried to flip from the expectations of a restaurant to a home, Jarek examined her blistered heel. "This is my mother and father, Fadey and Mary Jo Stepanov. This is the woman I told you about—Leigh Van Dolph. She needs first-aid cream and bandages."

"Yes, of course, honey." The woman's soft drawl spoke of a Southern influence. In a jade hostess gown, she smiled graciously. "Come with me—"

Her eyes were as green as Jarek's!

"I'll do it," Jarek stated as he held her ankle and began inspecting the blister closely. When his mother left the room to return with the supplies, he began cleaning the blister with an antiseptic tissue.

Leigh's briefcase fell to the floor, and her underwear and ruined hose tumbled out. But she was too stricken by the man who stood by the Stepanovs. He was very relaxed without his business suit, his shirtsleeves rolled up and a glass of wine in his hand. *His eyes the same shade of green as Jarek's!*

"You're Mikhail Stepanov." She stared at the older man and woman and blinked at the long, flowing, dark green dress of the woman, the man standing in his socks, very comfortable in his home. "Mr. and Mrs. Stepanov. This is your home."

"Of course," the man who was as tall as Jarek and Mikhail answered.

She considered the flames in the fireplace, which reflected on the rich wood paneling. This was a very comfortable home, with beautiful wooden furniture, gleaming hardwood floors, broken by thick, serviceable rugs. Earth, sea, and sky-colored pottery softened the room, the night and the Pacific sprawling in front of the massive windows.

"I believe you've met my brother, Jarek?" Mikhail's tone had just that hint of an accent. It matched Jarek's.

She studied the man kneeling in front of her. "You," she said finally. "You're his brother."

"I am—sometimes," Jarek agreed with one of those devastating grins. "He allows me to use the Amoteh for a showroom for our furniture. I work with Dad. Mikhail chose a different path, but at times, he helps out."

He seemed to be settling in to enjoy the fireworks, but Leigh wasn't ready for the explosion—just yet. She couldn't afford one, not with Mikhail so close and catchable.

Jarek was Mikhail Stepanov's brother, not a handyman. She could have killed him—placed her hands around that thick muscular throat and tightened slowly.... She'd actually offered him a tip!

"Welcome to our home," Fadey said, grinning broadly at her, and then at Jarek. Fadey's accent was pure immigrant. "Yes, she is a fine catch, I think. Not so skinny as most young women nowadays. Such pretty little curls, just as you said."

Fadey's gray eyes swept over Leigh. "And she appears to be strong, too. That is a good sign for—"

He grunted lightly as Mary Jo's elbow nudged his side and her look warned him. "Here," Fadey said with a chuckle in his tone, "let me take your shoes and place them by the fire to dry. I'll work with them later. A woman should have good shoes. But then my son might not be able to carry you, eh? A man likes to carry a woman sometimes."

This time Mary Jo's tone warned. "Fadey."

"Your home," she repeated and stared into Jarek's dark green eyes, while wishing to throw herself at him in a brawl, the same as she had when, as a child, the other children made fun of her parents. Instead she smiled tightly and tried to recover, which was difficult while stuffing her underclothes into her briefcase, the hose sliding free once more to mock her. She hurriedly stuffed them back in, trying for a panache that wasn't possible.

Jarek rose to take the briefcase from her, placing it on the chair as he tugged her to her feet. His eyes locked with hers as Mary Jo said, "We're so glad you could come to dinner. Jarek has told us so much about you."

"He has? I mean—yes, of course."

Yes, of course. She'd only slept in the same bed with him. He'd watched her yawn and stretch and—and he'd smoothed her thigh.

Mikhail extended his hand, taking hers. The height and the power and the smile were there, the likeness to Jarek. But Mikhail was smoothly polished, a businessman compared to the pirate, Jarek. "I understand that you wanted to meet me? I'm sorry about the mixup in our appointments. Perhaps tonight we can enjoy my mother's Tex-Mex cooking, and at my office tomorrow, we can discuss business. You can find me when you are rested and comfortable. Please accept my offer of a courtesy room at the Amoteh until our business is concluded."

Stunned at so easily making arrangements with Mikhail, Leigh struggled to recover as Jarek eased away her damp suit jacket. "Oh, I couldn't do that, but I would—"

"As my guest. Do not refuse me this pleasure, please," Mikhail said smoothly, gallantly.

"I guess I could. Yes, thank you. That would be nice.... Ah, this is very nice. How nice. Yes, nice. An invitation to dinner in your home. Quite nice."

She jerked her head away from Jarek's prowling finger. He lightly tugged at her hair, like a boy enchanted with a new toy, or—Leigh shivered at the look—or a man who had just brought a woman home to introduce her to his parents. "It gets curlier when it's damp and it smells like flowers."

She stared at him, at Mikhail who was smiling softly, then at Fadey and Mary Jo. "Yes, I'm afraid I'm not very presentable. I apologize."

With a look that said she'd assessed the situation, Mary Jo moved closer to place her arm around Leigh. "No, honey. My men do need to behave. They're the ones who need to apologize. It's apparent that you didn't know you were being invited to meet the entire family. Why don't you come with me into the kitchen and we can talk a bit, without them? I understand you're a wonder with sales and marketing know-how. How interesting that must be. I have a little office here and market Fadey's furniture with catalogs and brochures. We have a Web site, too, but the boys manage that. Maybe you could give me some business tips.''

Mary Jo's ''boys'' were towering, powerful men. Leigh glanced at Jarek, who stood in the shadows now, his expression closed and thoughtful.

His mother followed that look, locked to Leigh, and then took her arm. ''Come along, darlin'. My menfolk are a little overpowering, standing together like that, two of them grinning like loons, the other—well, honey, the other doesn't know quite what is happening, or what to do about it. I hope you like Tex-Mex food. It's just the thing for a cold, rainy day like today. I used to travel, too, in the early days, when Fadey's furniture needed to be out there in display rooms. Jarek does that now at the Amoteh. I enjoy our home now, but it was a delight to show off my husband's wonderful work. My parents bought enough to fill their home, and a few relatives, too. Fadey didn't want to sell to them, and there were edges to be soothed in those first days, but we managed.''

Fadey shook his head and his closed expression, so like Jarek's, said he was brooding. ''Her father didn't think I was worthy, a no-account immigrant—''

Mary Jo's low easy laughter filled the room. ''But I did, and that's what counted, darlin'.''

Leigh looked over her shoulder to Jarek. When she could have a private moment with him, she would tell him exactly what she thought—

Then his expression changed from withdrawn and thoughtful to sultry. His body seemed to tense, poised and corded, and the hair on Leigh's nape lifted warningly. A wave of sensation seemed to wash from him, curling around her, taking her breath away and making her skin tighten, her cheeks flush.

She could almost feel him breathe, feel him close to her, touching her, though the spacious room separated them.

He rubbed his chest as if soothing an ache there, and Leigh, just for a moment, wanted to comfort him—but then, she had her own problems, didn't she?

If he made her uneasy, she'd just have to deal with him.

And the first item on her list was to tell him that his little joke wasn't funny at all—as a woman who had to take care of herself, and her pride, Leigh was set to tell him off at the first chance.

Three

————

"So quiet?" Jarek asked lightly as he slid the magnetic key card into the lock of the Seawind Suite. He opened the door, flipped on the light switch and carried Leigh's laptop computer and small travel-worn luggage bag inside.

The luxurious suite, the fresh flowers on the hallway table, the sumptuous contemporary furniture, and the magnificent view of the ocean's night startled Leigh, waylaying her plans to set Jarek straight.

She followed him into the softly lit suite, watched him crouch to light the small fireplace. When the flames began to rise, Jarek indicated the small but complete office space near the window. "You should have everything you need there. You must have impressed my brother—this suite is reserved for only his best contacts."

Jarek stood with his back to the fire, his tall, powerful body outlined in the flickering firelight and again that tension that Leigh didn't understand leaped to life. "I make you nervous," he said slowly, studying her.

Leigh wouldn't admit the sensations he could cause, by a look, by a light touch with those broad, callused hands. She kicked off her shoes, which Fadey had treated to oils and polishing, and walked to the windows. She crossed her arms and decided to go for equaling her tab with Mr. Jarek Stepanov. His brooding looks at dinner said he was considering an issue, and didn't like the final answers coming back to him.

Neither had she. He was out to flirt with her, and he was too risky. She didn't like risks or surprises and he was dangerously full of both. She had obligations and business, and she feared what lurked between them.

In the cab of his pickup as they had returned to the resort, Leigh had felt very small and uncertain. "Amoteh means strawberry in the Chinook language, isn't that right?"

"There are strawberries here, yes."

"On Strawberry Hill? I heard about it today. The inlet by that big, black rock that widens with the tide and creates an island from that peninsula. They say that long ago, in whaling days, an enslaved Hawaiian swam to shore as the ship wrecked. He cursed the island because he knew he was dying there and not his homeland."

The air had been close and tense and too silent. Jarek seemed grim, a contrast to her earlier impression of him as a flirt, a lady-killer. "You like my family, then?" he had asked in the old-fashioned phrasing that Fadey had used.

"They seem nice. Solid." The Stepanovs had made a good home for their family, settling into a life that blended Fadey's heritage and Mary Jo's Texan background. The combination was of laughter, passion, teasing and deep love. Mary Jo had the easy manners of a woman bred to society, managing the towering, powerful Stepanov males easily. Elegant, lithe and graceful, she was taller than Leigh's more curved and compact body. The graceful chignon of blond tempered with gray was smooth in contrast to Leigh's unruly curls, and clearly Fadey's passion for his wife, his pride in her, had not dimmed. Each look spoke of love and commitment. "Your mother is very beautiful—a beauty queen, wasn't she? Raised on a huge cattle ranch?''

"Yes. We have cousins in Texas. They come here sometimes. In fact, we have cousins everywhere. My father's brothers emigrated at the same time.''

Now, with Jarek looking at her in that odd, intent and brooding way, those jutting eyebrows drawn together as if he was seeing something in her that he didn't like, Leigh decided it was time to make certain he understood—

One dark look at his lips caused her to tremble, then she forced herself back to the task of making certain that Jarek knew that he didn't fit into her agenda. She didn't want to think about those sensuous lips prowling over hers, evoking more than the clang of warning bells. He was too close, too big, and had already affected her too much, her senses taut, aware of him. "Get this straight—I don't trade off sexual favors for business deals.''

"You insult me," he said slowly, deeply, in the stiff, old-fashioned way that she had noticed in Fadey and Mikhail. Mary Jo's Texan drawl blended the deep tones, the foreign phrasing, yet that accent was there—and now it was too quiet, arrogant and bristling.

She pivoted to look at him. "It's how you look at me. There's no need to play games. I'm not buying. I've got enough on my plate without—without a man after summer conquests.''

She was tired, stunned by the warmth of the Stepanov home, the easy laughter and the love—the security. She was angry, too, Jarek's deception nettling her. "Very funny—letting me assume that Mikhail would be at a restaurant. I hope you had fun tonight, watching me flounder. I was very upset. I try to be poised, ready for business, and then, suddenly—there I was—in your family home. None of that pretense was necessary. I do not like surprises. I've had enough of them in my life.''

"You do not flounder and I didn't think you would come

to my parents'. You have enchanted my family. You might have preferred to sulk around the resort, trying to nab him. My brother can get very difficult. I have been lectured on how nice you are and how I must treat you well. You think I like this? I am thirty-six, not a boy.''

Clearly she had touched a masculine nerve, but she wasn't backing up. ''There's more to it than you wanting to make meeting Mikhail easier for me. You enjoyed your own private joke—letting me think that you were a handyman. And I think that Mikhail deliberately avoided me today, so that he could enjoy your little surprise. You were in cahoots with him.''

''We both prefer to work alone sometimes,'' Jarek said quietly. ''Mikhail saw you when he wanted, how he wanted. Or he wouldn't have seen you at all.''

''As a favor to you?''

''It's no worse than you asking me to introduce you at a restaurant and then leave.''

All evening she had sensed undercurrents from him, deep, dark brewing storms that his family understood. She'd caught the silent exchanges between Jarek and his family. But she was here to do business. His problems were his own; she had enough of her own, she thought desperately. ''And you're set to make me pay for something I didn't do and don't comprehend.''

His eyes narrowed in the shadows and the planes of his face caught the dim night. ''To the point then, Ms. Top Sales Guru of Bella Sportswear— You are wearing a bikini beneath your clothing.''

''Yes. We've already discussed that. It's one of Bella's best models and made of the best fabric. It's very brief, spaghetti straps, adjustable triangular cups conforming to every breast shape and reinforced to support full-figured women, ties at the hips, and a cotton crotch lining. Done in Tahitian floral of blue, greens, or reds, it—''

His hand sliced through the shadows, stopping her. He shook his head, then rammed his hand through his hair, glaring

at her. "What do you think it does to a man to know that—
to know that one tug of a bow could bring into his hands the
soft flesh he desires, that the 'cotton crotch' protects what he
would have as his own?"

Leigh breathed unevenly, trying to leap from telling Jarek
exactly what she thought of his little joke, of his intimate,
shocking statement. She preferred to blandly divert the conversation, waylaying any pursuit of her. He'd rethink his interest in her and back off when he saw that she wasn't susceptible, or interested.

She stepped into her diversion. "I'm missing the message
here. Are you telling me that I should consider a marketing
plan for your brother, based on male preferences?"

"No." The curt answer slapped at her. He sighed raggedly
and shook his head again. "No, do not do that. I think I should
go. I wish you luck tomorrow. My brother is a very, very good
businessman. Georgia will have your breakfast ready in the
morning. Please do not upset her. Mikhail has called the staff
and they have prepared this room for you. The refrigerator is
stocked. You will find what office machines and supplies that
you will need."

She didn't want to appear ungrateful—after all, she had met
Mikhail and she would soon leave. She reached out to lay her
hand on his arm. "I do appreciate the introduction, if not the
method. Thank you."

Jarek stared at her hand on his sleeve. "I can't move," he
said unevenly, his gaze shifting to lock with hers.

The impact took her breath away. Then Jarek sighed raggedly again and slowly, so slowly lowered his lips to hers.
With her eyes open, she saw his close, saw the intense expression, the line between his brows. The gentle, brief pressure
of his lips wasn't a kiss, but that of an exploration, tasting her.

While she stood, held by the impact of that slight kiss, Jarek
groaned deeply, unevenly and shook his head. In another moment, he was gone, the door closing softly behind him.

Leigh stood still for a long time, trying to understand what she felt, the rustle of something so deep and poignant that it frightened her. Even lying on the luxurious bed, the ocean's waves lulling her, she couldn't push away the restlessness that had never before plagued her—she'd always slept easily, anywhere, anytime, and now—

Leigh flopped to one side and remembered how Jarek had looked lying next to her—that slumberous, sensual look that took in her body, the way he touched her cheek.

He was just what she didn't need. Not now. Not one more complication in her life. Tomorrow she'd sell Mikhail on the idea of a Bella shop at the Amoteh, then she'd check on her parents and—

She had to keep her focus. Her family depended on her.... Leigh slid into sleep with the taste of Jarek's kiss on her lips.

At sunset the next day, Jarek stood on the shore, watching the tide ease away, leaving the smooth sand, the strands of tangled seaweed and driftwood. He braced his legs against the strong cold wind that tore his opened shirt away from his chest, leaving it to the rain's chill.

He should have been tired, working to make up the time he'd lost at the shop, and one man had stayed home with his sick wife. Fadey's employees knew that he placed family first and work second.

The company was growing, the quality of Stepanov furniture had produced a fine reputation. His mother's catalog and marketing had placed Stepanov pieces in some of the finest showrooms.

Jarek smiled briefly when thinking of how Mary Jo preferred her small neat home office to the wild Russian music Fadey loved while he worked, the sawdust and the clutter, punctuated by yelling—not in anger, but to music. In the early years, she had placed her sons in a playpen while she helped Fadey work.

The Amoteh's rooms weren't completely filled with Stepanov furniture yet and Mikhail's goal was to have every room as a showcase, replacing the standard hotel furniture. A hard work schedule hadn't stopped Fadey from grinning at Jarek as the sawdust flew between them, the saw humming in the vast workshop and passionate Russian music over it all. "You like this girl, eh? You bring her home to meet your parents. That is good. You bring her again, and maybe next time she'll let you sit by her. Maybe next time, those eyes won't flash so with anger as she looks at you. Still, a woman does not always like a man to carry her around, you know. Young women in business now are peculiar. Still, I like her. Mikhail says he has big plans for her—what does he mean, eh? Maybe he wants her for himself? Hey! Where are you going? I want to talk more about this little girl you brought home—"

"I don't," Jarek had said curtly. He didn't want to think of his brother and Leigh. Both focused on business, they would understand each other immediately. They were compatible; he wasn't. "She's here to do business with Mikhail, that's all."

Fadey had studied his son slowly. "No, I do not think that is all. Perhaps it is time for you to come alive, eh? To feel a man's passion at the first sight of a woman, like I did your mother? Sometimes it comes at a man like that. Knocks him into love before he can put up a good fight."

Then his big arms had enclosed Jarek and Fadey kissed his cheeks. "You have much love in you, my son. Enough for another woman. You think about that, eh?"

On the beach, Jarek breathed slowly, searching what ran inside him, the desire for Leigh fighting for the love he still held for Annabelle. He picked up the shell of a razor clam and ran his thumb over the cold smooth interior. Called "moss back" because of its size and age, the clam had been dug improperly, the meat ruined.

The seamless safety of his life, day by day, had also been broken. By a woman whose skin had been warm beneath his touch, whose eyes were soft brown or honey-gold according to her mood—a feeling woman, struggling to keep her family safe.

She seemed to think only of them, how she could manage to care for them—the woman with fire in her coppery hair and with lips that were soft and pink without lipstick or guile— the woman with the scent that set his desire humming.

How could he explain to anyone how much he had wanted to bring her home to meet his family?

How could he explain, when he didn't understand himself, the need to fasten his lips to hers and feed the passion within him?

In the distance, Deadman's Rock soared in the sunset, black and deadly, reminding Jarek of the love he'd lost. Then he saw a small figure in the distance, huddled against the wind and rain.

Nothing could have kept him from making his way to her.

Leigh didn't acknowledge him as he walked by her side, moving slightly to shelter her from the full blast of the cold wind. She looked like a child in the overlarge, cheap plastic raincoat, the hood hiding her face.

"Problems?" he asked lightly, and wished he didn't care. He wished he hadn't seen through the raincoat to that tight black sweater and pants, the wind pushing the plastic against her body.

"Big ones," she answered curtly and added, "Your brother is a big problem. He's smooth and he's tough."

Jarek nodded; he knew exactly how tough Mikhail could be—never showing how much he hurt after his wife divorced him. "How did your meeting go?"

As if she were too weary battling the world, Leigh plopped down on a driftwood log. "Good. Up to a point. He wants me to set up and run the Bella Shop. But there is a price tag. Once I mentioned that Morris was expecting me back at work, he asked a few questions about my boss and my job, and then he said, 'You or no deal.' But I do strictly sales. I'd have to learn the shop business from the ground up. Oh, I can do that—I've held enough jobs to swing learning another one, but—"

Jarek sat and stretched his legs out beside hers. He liked

the look of them, side by side, a woman's and a man's. "How's the blister?"

"Peachy. I don't understand Mikhail's interest in how old Morris was, or if he was married, or—"

Jarek understood immediately. Mikhail was very thorough, and he'd caught something Jarek had missed—Leigh's emotional attachment to another man. "How old is he?"

"Morris? Seasoned. Ageless. He's a very nice man. He's given me a lot, taught me a lot. We work closely and sometimes travel together. He's very protective of me. Mikhail's interest in whether we worked at the office or in Morris's condominium seemed quite irrelevant, and what we ate, and so forth. None of that has anything to do with why I should manage the shop at the resort. I worked hard to be where I am, and this would be a career demotion."

Leigh liked Morris. That fact nagged at Jarek. "Is Morris married?"

She shrugged and said, "It doesn't matter, but he's never married. I've worked in shops before since I could barely reach a cash register, so that isn't a problem. I know inventory management and display, and Morris will see that I have everything I need. He's very good at understanding my limits. I'm still not happy, by the way, at the way you carried me into your parents' home like a sack of feed. Or your little joke. Someday, I just may pay you back."

Jarek understood Mikhail's questioning perfectly; Mikhail was testing the depth of the relationship between Leigh and her boss, and he'd come up with a plan to keep her near and away from Morris. "Any other problems?"

Leigh's sigh said there were. "Only my parents. Morris lets me have time off on a moment's notice to deal with their problems—which are many. He knows them, and he's very indulgent. Not many employers would have understood my family. Your brother doesn't seem to be very movable on some issues. He wants me in that shop every day, committed to it, and he wants status reports. He's an 'in' to other Mignon

Resort managers, a trendsetter. He knows exactly how to toss his weight around, ever so unstated. But the bottom line is, if I don't play his way, the whole project is down the tubes, and that nice fat bonus Morris promised me with it.''

She shook her head and pushed the toes of her canvas shoes into the wet sand. A gust of wind swept the plastic hood from her face and a flurry of curls stormed around her face. ''I don't know why I'm telling you all this.''

He wanted to help her, to see her laugh and play and relax. ''Maybe I could influence Mikhail to—''

She turned, her eyes narrowing at him. He thought they were the color of the sun dancing on the waves, with all those rich currents and depth below. A man who enjoyed the battle of nature, its rage and its calm, Jarek felt that same fierce pleasure as she focused upon him. Concerned with business, Leigh's focus wasn't that easily distracted, but for the moment, he had her attention.

''Don't you dare interfere with this project. I handle my own business,'' she stated firmly.

''Oh, how well I know.''

Seeming to be satisfied with that, she turned back to study the ocean and Jarek found himself captivated by the line of her throat, the sweep of her lashes, the wind in her hair, which brought her fragrance curling around him—*that woman scent.*

Leigh seemed unaware of the tension in him. ''If my parents decide to follow the winds of the universe, anything could happen to them. They love me and I love them, but Ed needs rest and a doctor's care. Bliss is aging and still thinks tie-dying will pay for what they need. She forgets to take her calcium, then there's those wild moods and sometimes depression brought on by menopause. The van needs repair and that means more bills they can't pay. They're likely to drive it anyway, out to the desert or to the mountains, and my brother—well, Ryan will never grow up. I can't manage their needs and build the shop at the Amoteh. I've got to get back to my room and try to extract a promise from my parents that they will just stay in one place until I can manage this whole thing.''

She pushed off the log and stood, her fists jammed into the plastic pockets. ''I don't know why I'm telling you all this. Dinner was nice last night—despite the mistaken idea that I would meet Mikhail at a restaurant. Gee, I wonder where I would get that idea from. But thanks. It must have been wonderful to grow up as you and Mikhail did—in one place.''

''It was.'' Jarek stood and lifted the rain hood over her hair, smoothing it as it curled around his fingers. Why did she entrance him? Why did he want to gather her close and protect her?

Her wary brown gaze, shielded by those fabulous lashes, slid up to search his face—trying to see past flesh and bone and into the truth of him. For a moment, everything that Jarek loved—the ocean, the wind and salty air caught and tangled around him. There in the sound of the crashing waves, the wind tearing at him, he wondered what it would be like to hold her, skim his hands over that soft warm flesh, and make love to her.

Leigh tensed as if she, too, felt the startling sensual impact. She stood back from him, her hands clasping the raincoat firmly around her. ''I've got to go. I've got work to do,'' she said unevenly as she turned and hurried back along the shoreline.

What was it that had startled her? Did he wrongly imagine that she had—just for that instant—leaned toward him?

Jarek rubbed his hand against his jaw. Perhaps he saw, just in that instant, something he wanted, rather than reality. Keeping his distance, he followed her past the old piers lashed together by cable and up the winding wooden steps to the Amoteh. When she slid the card into the lock and entered her room, Jarek turned to find Mikhail's grin.

Immaculately dressed in a navy suit, Mikhail always seemed to know everything, especially things a younger brother might not want to reveal. When Leigh's door closed, Mikhail leaned a shoulder against the wall, clearly settling in to question Jarek. "So you're really interested, are you?"

"Are you?" he asked as he walked by his brother. He saw no reason to spare his suspicions of Mikhail's motives.

Mikhail's brows raised at the growling edge to Jarek's question and he swung into stride beside him. "Yes, I am. She's driven and alone and exhausted. And she interests my brother enough that he follows her through a storm to see that she is safe. Because she is a guest, I must, of course, make certain that she is safe from my brother."

Mikhail's cool, methodical mind could at times intuitively sense Jarek's moods and that nettled. An older brother's appraisal was not always wanted, and now Jarek prowled through very private emotions. He'd loved one woman and lost her; he didn't think he could desire again, yet he did. "I came to check on the showroom. I may have left a window open. The carpet could be ruined by the rain."

"Sure. Try another one. And while you're at it, think about the man who is after her. He's sent flowers to her. So she's informed him that she's staying here. Her telephone has been busy most of the day, and she requested more paper for the suite's fax machine. She can work, I give her that. And she's pushy when she wants something, like letting someone else manage the shop here. I'm rather enjoying the sparring. She's very good, a detailist. But she's afraid, terribly afraid of failing—something I understand, without an obvious statement from her."

"She has a family she loves very much and they depend on her…. Has she eaten?" Jarek remembered how she had devoured yesterday's breakfast. Leigh was so focused on her goals that she may have forgotten.

Mikhail shrugged and studied his brother. "Why don't you ask her? She's got you scared, doesn't she? You're afraid that you might want her enough, and that you'll come to life. That was quite some entrance you made last night, carrying her into the folks' house as if she were already yours. This should be interesting, because I don't sense that she knows very much about her own needs—except to succeed, and there is more to life than that.''

He rarely spoke of needs and Jarek wondered if Mikhail's lonely hours were filled with regrets, a man alone who had wanted a family.

Then Mikhail said, ''By the way, here is the address where her parents are staying. She's called them apparently, and the message got waylaid before being passed on to her. I just happened to notice.''

Jarek glanced at the address on the paper Mikhail had handed him. He knew that Mikhail's finely tuned staff didn't make mistakes. Mikhail had wanted more information on the girl in the Seawind Suite. ''I like to know who I'm doing business with. In this case, it's a woman who has caught my brother's interest, and she's so focused on what she has to do, the consequences of her failure, and concerned for her family, that she—''

''Lay off.'' With his brother's chuckle following him, Jarek turned and walked out of the luxurious resort into the full blast of a spring squall.

The force of the wind and the chilling rain did not ease his need to see Leigh again, to hold her.

The quiet pain inside him warned—he'd loved and lost that love. While his body might desire Leigh, he would guard his heart.

Leigh finished changing her appointment schedule, no easy task as she assigned an up-and-coming, very hungry sales assistant to meet with prospective clients, catalog buyers and suppliers. She'd seen Megan's corporate-climber type before, the I'm-your-replacement eagerness to learn.

Ten days of shuffling appointments, trying to sway Mikhail into letting someone else handle the Bella shop, had been frustrating. Morris, as usual, was not worried, completely confident that she would work out the details to Bella's good.

The memory of Jarek's light kiss, the way his sea-green eyes had cruised her body and had heated it, disturbed her nights.

She hadn't seen him since that night in the rain. Perhaps he'd decided that she was a no-go, that she wasn't interested in a summer romance and he'd moved on. But had she?

She frowned at the fax scrolling out of the machine provided with the suite, and skimmed the Bella corporate sales figures on it. Accessories were down—the wrap-around sunglasses yielding to oversize styles, clear tote bags favored in lieu of straw ones, the roll-up straw beach blanket made progress and so did the large crushable straw hat.

Leigh traced the sales figures graph on the new line of men's swimwear and they were not encouraging.

Nor were her brother's and parents' bills, which she had had mailed to her.

She watched the thundering ocean waves in the distance, a layer of fog rolling in at early evening.

Mikhail Stepanov was a tough, slick businessman. He was courteous, yet never budged an inch. She sensed he was enjoying the power struggle between them. Her efforts to sway him into having someone else manage the Bella shop had slid away like the rain on the window. In a strategic move to apply slight pressure, Leigh had had boxes of Bella Sportswear shipped to the Amoteh. She hoped that once Mikhail saw the boxes, the goods waiting to be sold, he would—

A flash of color caught her eye, a big, slow-moving rusty van, splashed with hot-pink flowers and flags pulled into the parking lot. Bundles and poles had been lashed to the top.

The van was too familiar and when Leigh saw Jarek emerge from the driver's side, she closed her eyes. Memories of Ed and Bliss's arrival during her past business deals scampered through her mind— "He's brought them here. I'll kill him."

She hurried out of the suite and down the lush, quiet corridor. Her heart pounded as the elegant elevator swooped to the lower floor. If she could just catch them in time, she could arrange for Ed and Bliss to stay away from the Amoteh—not that she didn't love them, but business and her family had never mixed.

"Precious Blossom," Ed exclaimed lovingly as he and Bliss both hugged Leigh, their arms around each other.

"Oh, my sweet little baby," Bliss crooned and ran her thin hands over Leigh's face. She arranged a fresh flower coronet over Leigh's curls. "You've got that stressed look. You're all worried. I can feel those awful stressed vibes. You shouldn't work so hard. Are you doing your yoga faithfully? And meditating? Oh, you have that look that says you haven't been doing either and you've lost your center. You know how important it is to focus on centering, on aligning your chakras, Precious Blossom."

Leigh's center consisted of keeping the family bills paid. She could have cried—her parents were getting older and their clothes were shabby, and Bliss's usually placid face had new lines. Ed's usual ponytail seemed even more thin, probably due to his recent appendectomy. In Leigh's arms, her parents seemed frail and thin. She hugged them again.

"I love you," she whispered, meaning it with all her heart and soul. They were so dear and loving and she treasured them. "Ed, are you feeling all right?"

"No, he's not," Bliss answered, the tone unusually sharp for her. "If Jarek hadn't taken care of repairing the van and driving, we would have never gotten here. Ed requires more sleep than he used to, and he gets grumpy. He slept all the way."

Ed scowled at her. "Me? Grumpy? I didn't sleep all the way."

"You did so."

"Your parents are tired. Let's go in," Jarek said quietly at her side.

She turned to him, fear raising the hair on her nape. "'In?' *In the Amoteh, you mean?*"

"They have a reservation." Jarek studied her parted lips,

her wide eyes and reached to tug her hair. With a boyish grin, he added, "Precious Blossom."

She shook her head and closed her eyes. Images of the Amoteh's pricey bill sickened her. His grin said he knew everything—even that her parents had never married formally. *And her mother had probably hauled out her favorite albums—little Precious Blossom playing nude and happy!*

"Maybe there is another place. Somewhere that they would be more comfortable. I'll make some calls—they like campgrounds better. Don't you, Ed? Bliss?" she began with more haunting images of past ruined business deals zipping through her mind.

There was that time when Bliss had taken aside a potential chain buyer's mistress and had lectured her on her self-worth and personal esteem. The endowed "personal assistant" had taken Bliss's advice and vacated, leaving the buyer enraged; he'd immediately canceled the tenuous deal that would have filled a clothing chain stores' racks with Bella swimwear.

Morris hadn't said anything then. But when Ed, dressed in his meditation gown, had passed out worry stones at a dressy business convention in which she represented Bella, Morris had suggested that perhaps she leave her family at home.

Jarek reached to haul her parents' worn duffel bag from the top of the van. "You'll probably want to catch up. Let's go in. Ed and Bliss need a good warm room and Georgia has prepared a special meal for them. I'll bring in their bags and then see about heating it up."

While Leigh stood in the rain and tried to deal with her parents' frailty, her emotions and the business deal that meant a hefty bonus, Jarek leaned over and kissed her. "Everything will work out fine. You'll see."

Leigh grabbed his black sweatshirt in her fist. "Let's talk about that after I've killed you. I really don't like surprises. I haven't planned for this."

"Precious Blossom has never liked surprises. I don't know why. All of life is a surprise," Ed stated. "She's not violent at all. She wouldn't really kill you. She just talks that way to Winter Child sometimes. Our son and Precious Blossom couldn't be more different, but they both have loving hearts. And that's the most important thing in the universe, to have a loving heart."

Jarek's expression said he was withholding a grin, and Ed and Bliss beamed at Leigh. She would deal with Jarek's tendency to surprise her later. She loved them, and they were hers, and they needed her and rest— "Let's go in, shall we?" she asked, linking her arms with theirs.

When Jarek opened the door to the brisk knocking at nine o'clock that night, Leigh flung herself into the room with the force of the wind howling around his home. "You should have answered your telephone. It would have saved me a trip. You can't hide from me or what you've done. The flowers painted on the van look real cute next to your brother's black BMW."

The wind caught the towel around Jarek's hips and chilled the water beading his body. He closed the door behind her. "I was probably taking a shower when you called."

"Don't give me excuses."

He swept a hand in front of the damp towel he was wearing knotted around his hips and indicated his damp hair.

"All right. Maybe that's a possibility," Leigh admitted. "Your hair is wet and you smell like soap."

His body tightened as she watched a trail of water slowly wind down his chest. Jarek impatiently swept the droplet from his hardened nipple; he didn't like being so responsive to those fascinating gold eyes.

Leigh scowled up at him and tore aside the plastic hood sheltering her face. She blew away the drop of water at the end of her nose. "What have you done now?" she demanded, her hands on her hips.

Leigh waved her hands. "You just do things, don't you? And you don't think of the repercussions? You brought my parents here, and now *Ed and Bliss are in the Amoteh. In one of the rooms!*''

''I hope they are comfortable.'' Jarek rubbed his hand over his bare chest and found the ache that Leigh always brought. It wasn't a sad ache, rather a happy little glow. Did he really want that light, boyish feeling? he brooded. He'd had that once, and fate had taken away the woman he'd loved.

Leigh tore off the raincoat and tossed it onto the floor. Dressed in a black sweat suit, she faced him once more. ''I've just spent the last four days trying to keep up with Bella's regular work at the main office—the first of June is great last-minute selling season, you know. We ran out of flyers for a top merchandiser's catalog, size ten and twelve seems to be understocked, I'm working on inventory control and fall sales right now…and *now Ed and Bliss are right here. Right here!*''

She waved her hands again, and Jarek enjoyed the graceful, if frustrated, feminine flourishes. He enjoyed watching her pace back and forth in his home, frowning fiercely, struggling to right the ship she perceived he had sunk. ''You and your surprises. They are *not* welcome in my life. I don't like surprises. They never turn out well. Once your brother finds Bliss tie-dying T-shirts and trying to sell them to the guests, and Ed playing his flute and giving everyone advice on how to go with the flow, all the work I've been doing to convince Mikhail that I am right about the shop will be ruined. He'll just want all of us out of here.''

Leigh took a deep breath and sailed on in her tirade. ''I've spent hours trying to keep them out of Georgia's kitchen and away from Mikhail. He dropped in anyway and seemed to be enjoying himself. Ed gave him a worry stone and some love beads. Your brother won't enjoy himself when he finds dye in the bathtub. Ed and Bliss are both sleeping now. They're exhausted and they badly need the rest. *I'm* exhausted, and I've got to find a way to get them out of here without hurting their feelings.''

She flopped to the brown woven couch, legs sprawled on

the floor and placed her hand over her eyes. "Your brother has been acting like a host, not a potential Bella partner. Why me? Why me? Why does he want me, specifically, to design the Bella shop and work it through the busy part of the season? Morris needs me. I can't do it. *And now you felt you could invite yourself into my life and personally chauffeur my parents here. How dare you!*"

"Tell me about Morris," Jarek said quietly, wanting to know more about the man who held Leigh's friendship, and perhaps her heart.

She sighed dramatically and singsonged an answer. "We went through this before. And there was Mikhail's little inquisition about Morris, too. Morris is wonderful, kind, understanding, a quiet, beautiful man who is very thoughtful. He says he's working on getting married. I hope he does. I have no idea who she is."

She lifted her head to glare at him. "You're trying to distract me. I don't like it. You had no right to enter my life and bring my parents here. I was going to finish this deal and then check on them. It's hard keeping up with them."

Jarek had a good idea of who Morris might be considering as his future wife. The thought nagged at him. "You love your parents. I saw it earlier."

"Of course. They're wonderful. They just don't understand business and I'm responsible for everyone. Oh, they looked so worn. Did you see how Ed favored his right side? And Bliss just looks as if she could drop. I can't bear to see them like that. I just wish I could make everything right for them."

"You are, I think. Doing your best."

"My best isn't good enough. I have little or no money to cope with my family, the last incident almost wiped out my savings—and I had to borrow to pay Ed's medical bills. I'm failing them."

"You're not. You're loving them and they know it."

Leigh surged out of the couch, stalked around the room barely noting the spartan furnishings, then looked out the win-

dow facing the ocean. She glanced at the small shelf holding
a picture of Annabelle and Jarek grinning into the camera. The
rest of the photos were stashed in a locked room at the furniture shop; he couldn't bear to look at them, to remember.
Echoes of Annabelle's plea curled inside him— *Come with
me…we'll make our baby. The time is right….*

But the time would never be right. Maybe Chief Kamakani's curse was true—

"Your wife?" Leigh asked, bringing him back through
time.

"Yes." Again, that quiet pain circled him, the image of the
empty boat floating back to shore.

Leigh's voice softened as her finger traced the frame. "I'm
sorry for your loss. I understand you loved her very much.
How difficult it must be to love so deeply and then— You
look tired, too. But then, flying down to San Francisco and
working on the van until it was roadworthy would do that to
a man, wouldn't it?"

So she'd noticed. A caring woman, wrapped in concern for
her parents, Leigh had also taken time to notice him. Jarek's
mood lightened suddenly. "Yes, Precious Blossom, it has been
quite the trip. Very informative, too."

She waved her hands furiously before speaking, "Oh! Oh!
Oh! 'Precious Blossom.' I've fought that name until I was of
an age to change it. Don't you dare tell anyone. I'm trying to
keep a business image and that name won't do at all."

Jarek shrugged, enjoying the color coming into her cheeks,
the way she tossed her head and the curls flew out like gleaming, copper-colored silk. She walked to him and shoved his
bare chest with the flat of her hand. "Now, you're trying to
derail me. I came here to say my piece. Just what do you think
you are doing? Ed and Bliss, here? You had no right. You are
in your busy season, too, and you took time to retrieve my
parents. Why?"

Jarek looked down at her, her hands on her hips as she
glared up at him. The heavy cloth over her breasts had tight-

ened, outlining the entrancing full shape. He ached to caress her, to smooth that fragrant skin, to taste the heat— "You should relax more."

She threw up her hands. "How? How? You don't know them. I love them, but I wish they would be more conventional. I wish they would realize that they are getting older and they need to take better care of themselves."

"They love you, very much. Now, with them near, you can settle into doing whatever you have to do for—Morris." On the three-day trip back in the van, Jarek had heard a little too much about how good Morris was to Leigh.

Leigh stared blankly at him. "I don't know who is more difficult to deal with—you or your brother. He's at least predictable. You're not."

He smoothed back her hair and cradled her face in his hand. "They love you, Leigh. Is that so bad?"

Tears filled her eyes as she shook her head. "They're like children, you know. Loving, trusting, enjoying every little slice of life. They need to be protected. I can't tell you how many con-men have taken advantage of them. But they never see the bad side of life, of what could happen, Jarek. I'm worried for them. They can't live in a van all their lives."

"Is that so wrong?" Jarek asked softly as he framed her face with his hands.

She frowned up at him, her hands clenching his forearms. "How would you know? Try having children for parents and try growing up in a van and changing schools more times than you can remember. Then there's the other side—trying to look like everyone else, when you weren't— If Ed and Bliss start showing off those naked childhood pictures of me in a place where I am trying for a business image, I'll—"

"You looked like a very happy child, a joyous, wild, free child who held life's song in her small hand. You looked as if you were well loved."

She studied him intently, then shoved away from him. "Yeah, well, life and necessities change people. There are realities, you know. And bills. They showed you the pictures already, didn't they?''

"Parents do that. Are you ashamed of your parents?" Jarek asked and watched those gold eyes flash with anger.

"No, of course not. I love them deeply. I know they love me. I've never doubted that love, and in that way, I had more than some children who had everything wealth could buy. I know of people who have lived in expensive houses, and haven't had one drop of the love and care that I had. But they're not the normal set of parents—you know, responsible, bill-paying, settled parents. They have no retirement income. Bliss thinks her T-shirt tie-dying is paying the bills. Ed's worry stones and love beads bring in pennies. Sometimes they give everything away. That's how much into reality they are.''

Her hand went to flatten against her chest. "I earn the money in the family, Jarek. I manage all the little details of my parents' and my brother's lives, and my own, when I can. I can't help it, but I get tired and grumpy and things don't go right when I'm flying all over the place trying to settle their problems. If they could just find a place to settle into. You know, like a retirement village with good medical care. But they'd never have that, oh no. Not Ed and Bliss. They want to be free. Someday, they'll die in a desert or a communal shack before I can get to them. I just couldn't bear anything happening to them. I love them."

"Well, now, they're here, and you're here." Jarek moved closer, needing to comfort and hold Leigh near. "And you're here, and I'm here."

"I know. They're here, and I should be glad to see them, but I'm trying so hard—oh, I hate this," she whispered unevenly as she brushed away her tears. "I just love them so much, and at times, I feel so helpless to protect and keep them safe."

Jarek drew her into his arms, placed his chin over her head and enjoyed the soft warm curves of her body against his, the fragrance of her hair brushing his skin. He looked over her head to the framed picture, to Annabelle in his arms. That ache in his chest didn't come, warmed away by Leigh's body against his.

Leigh sagged against him and shook her head. "Sometimes...I just get very tired. I've got to get back. Ed sometimes does his shaman prayers in the nude, to be better in tune with nature—the balcony is a likely place."

She pushed back from him and clasped her hands. "Just, please...back out of our lives. You were raised by traditional parents and you have no idea of what I'm facing here. You've done enough damage. I'll find some way to piece this whole mess together. I always do."

"Leigh?"

"Huh? What?"

He smiled lightly, mocking himself—here she was, completely without a clue as to how much he wanted to ease away his towel and her sweat suit and make love to her. Not the easy, gentle kind, but the hot, taking, soul-satisfying, body exhausting, slightly dying after the heights, kind of lovemaking that wiped everything away in its wake.

He studied those light brown eyes with their long bottom lashes, the pixieish way she frowned up at him, those soft curls spiraling along her cheek. He saw her as she had been in the photographs—a little girl, grinning at the camera, carefree and wild and natural.

He saw her as a woman struggling to hold her family safe.

He saw her as the woman he desired, her body heating and calling to his.

"Precious Blossom, I really need your full attention for this," he murmured as he leaned down to kiss her.

Four

As Jarek's mouth roamed hers, warm and firm and tempting, Leigh stood very still. The sensation that she was floating in sunlight bound her, then a heartbeat later, a wave of heat and hunger slammed into her.

His light kisses slid to the corners of her lips, tasting and nibbling them, to her cheek and to her ear, which he nuzzled slowly, effectively, setting off tiny electric charges within her. The rhythm of his caressing hand on her arm warmed, seduced and caused an earthshaking quiet to envelop her—as if somewhere deep inside, a part of her knew and feared what would happen if she didn't move away.

That inviting seduction continued, wrapping and holding her in scents and sensations too magical to shatter. She tasted freedom and sunshine and mystery and joy—she tasted the edge of his hunger, dark and swirling and passionate, taut and hot and beckoning her to step out on that ledge and fly with him. Beneath her fingertips, the muscles of his arms slid firm and strong and magnificent.

Hers, she thought. *He was hers.* She focused on him completely, just as she did when she wanted a nice fat contract, summing up the total package and considering where to begin.

The total package was big, warm, delicious and exciting, filled with textures and scents. She just caught her breath when his lips fused firmly to hers, slanting for a tight fit, his body pressing close to hers. She had to taste, to experience him, the storms slamming against her demanded that they be fed. In fact, Jarek was that storm, all smooth shoulders and power and soapy scents and heat, and she longed to step into the fray, holding her own, matching the temptation hurled at her.

Jarek's body pressed close and intimate, his hands braced beside her head as she leaned against the wall. Was the tempest outside his home, or was that her heart? Her blood swooshed through her veins, the warmth curling inside her body. She sensed that she had to feed and revel in the taking of this one man.

She dug her nails slightly into that smooth warm skin, because Jarek wasn't leaving her, not now, not when she'd just discovered how to fly—Leigh hadn't expected the arching hunger of her body as his hand cruised slowly, firmly downward, finding her waist, caressing the indentation and curve of her hip.

She hadn't expected to wrap her arms around him, holding that sweet hunger tight within her, savoring it, as she opened her mouth to his foraging one, her body taut against his. The muscles of his back flexed as her hands opened on them, and a sigh slid around her, from her, one of pleasure and need, a woman's call to a man.

She wanted to dive into Jarek, to take everything. Easing beneath her sweatshirt, his hand spread warm and rough and big upon her waist. She released her breath and then realized she'd been holding it as his thumb cruised her breast.

One tug of Bella's Tahitian Nights bikini bow, tied in front, and Jarek groaned, the heat between them rising as he shuddered just once. His open hand slid around her breast, hard palm pressing lightly against the tender weight. His body stilled, tensed as he groaned lightly, rubbing gently, her hardened nipple in the exact center of his palm.

The erotic motion sent shock waves through her; they zipped down and around and softened and heated. She hadn't been touched intimately, and realized the uneven, helpless sound was that of her own.

Leigh had to touch him, to feel that hard jaw within her hands, the angles and planes of his. She had to slide her fingers through his untamed hair, capturing it. He stilled then, leaning slightly back, his eyes slitted, his head tilted with arrogance.

The tempest swirled and stilled her as she stared back at him, waiting, wondering, stunned at her own emotions. Whatever was happening now was honesty between a man and a woman. She feared, even as she wanted…. "It won't work, Jarek," she whispered over lips that tasted of him, slightly swollen and sensitive to his kisses.

"Won't it?" he asked quickly as he leaned to kiss her more softly, entrancing her with the sweetness.

"We're too different," she managed, foraging for reality when lost in dizzying pleasure as Jarek's hands smoothed her breasts, her stomach. She held on to his shoulders, lost amid tossing emotions. "This is no good. No good at all. You're one big surprise package and I've never been good at surprises. They upset me."

He chuckled at that, his mouth curving against her throat. "You're not upset now. It feels very right. Do you wear bikinis all the time?"

After a day of running after Mikhail, dressed in her business suit, she'd needed to remove her very-proper bra, a heavy-duty "minimizer" which made her clothing fit better. "I'm short on underclothes and I bounce when I—"

"You are all woman, that's for sure. All woman," Jarek repeated in a low, uneven voice. Then he eased her sweatshirt high, his expression darkening as he considered her breasts—

"Jarek!" Leigh shivered at the hot open hunger in his eyes,

consuming her. Every particle of him seemed poised to take—to take everything, and that frightened her. She had to hold herself together, to focus, because she wasn't certain she could give more of herself away.

She pushed away from him and faced the wall, tugging her sweatshirt down and holding it firmly in her fists. She didn't know if she were holding it tautly down because she feared what his touch could do to her—make her lose control...or if she didn't grip something, she'd jerk it up and press her sensitized body against his smooth chest, skin to skin. "I think we'd better stop," she said unevenly.

She could feel his desire, feel him breathe, the air seeming to compress and expand around her. Then Jarek's arms came around her, and with his face against her cheek, he lifted her. He carried her to the couch and dropped her upon it. "You're going to drive me crazy, and I'll probably enjoy every minute of it," he muttered darkly.

On her back, Leigh studied the man towering over her, his hands at his hips, the damp towel revealing the sturdy shape of his desire. "Oh," she managed, quite brilliantly she thought, when her body still ached and softened—

"You keep lying there like that, that string bikini tangled at your waist, and I just might take it as an invitation," he stated darkly.

"Me? Invite you?" She scrambled to her feet, tugged the bikini top free and jammed it into her sweatpants pocket. She forced herself to meet his dark frown, braced herself against the need to go to him, to leap upon him. The prowling savagery within herself stunned Leigh. She'd faced entire boardrooms filled with unfriendly potential clients without this much emotion and she wasn't certain of herself—or Jarek. "I'm not blushing. Don't say that I am. I never blush. It's just hot in here."

She wished she hadn't glanced down past that enticing navel, to where the towel did little to conceal his hardened, stirring body. She shivered and looked away, embarrassed by her need to touch and explore—

"Uh-huh." Jarek shook his head and walked into the kitchen enclosure, separated by a counter which concealed his lower body. From a stack of folded clothes, he took a pair of jeans. Still holding her gaze, he slung the towel over his shoulder and stepped into the jeans, tugging up the zipper. "Look, I'm tired. Too tired, and you're wound too tight. I wonder what would happen if you ever relaxed. Let's have this discussion another time, shall we?"

Leigh didn't like the rising pitch of her voice, or the see-sawing of her emotions. She'd just lost control in Jarek's arms and they both knew it; her body still hummed with the need to be closer to him. She couldn't afford to be interested in him. Her instincts told her to go for the best defense—an argument. "'Wound too tight?' 'Wound too tight?' I don't like the sound of that."

He shook his head. "When was the last time you relaxed, Leigh? Did something that you like to do, instead of filling schedules and obligations? When did you think of what you wanted—for yourself?"

Who was he to prowl through her life? To criticize her management of a life she had worked very hard to create? Why should she feel that he had that right? "I have a job. A very good paying job with a bonus just in my hand. I'm just running a little under pressure now, because someone—you, specifically—has interfered with my life. You don't understand what it is to—"

He drew on a denim jacket and slid his bare feet into loafers. "I'll walk you back to the Amoteh."

Despite her uncertain emotions, Leigh sensed that Jarek was fighting a darkness she couldn't understand.

"I got here by myself. I can leave by myself," she said as she jerked open the door. She walked onto his porch and slammed the door behind her.

Leigh hurried into the storm, running up the steps to the

Amoteh, as her body trembled, still heated from his, the heaviness in her breasts aching— She shook her head furiously and rubbed her hands together and still the textures and strength of Jarek remained.

She spoke to the wind, just as she had as a child with no one to listen to reason. "I can't afford to be involved in an affair, not now, not at this stage of my life. He's unpredictable, one minute boyish and the next, he's brooding over something I don't understand, and the next he's very erotic and delicious, and—I've no time to play games. I've got a full schedule as it is. I have a family depending on me. I—"

Then she turned to see Jarek, his legs braced against the wind that pulled his jacket open and away from his bare chest. The wind hurled his hair away from his face, and in the slashing rain, the hard planes held no softness.

The primitive impact of his desire hurled across the distance, carried on the wind, slamming into her with enough force to take away her breath. With enough strength to tug at her body, to remind her that she'd arched feverishly against him, her hands tethering his face to hers, her tongue meeting his, suckling it in an erotic invitation.

Leigh closed her eyes and trembled, riveted by that jolting memory. When she opened them again, the night and the rain was cold upon her hot cheeks.

She wanted to cry. She wanted to laugh, mocking herself, releasing the taut hunger within.

But she braced herself against the wind and turned to walk to the resort. She had obligations and a job to do, and Jarek wasn't on her menu.

The next afternoon, Leigh clasped her clipboard to her chest with one hand and held a mug of Amoteh's special house-blend coffee in the other. The strawberries on the mug had given her the idea for a special fabric, sold only at the resort, an inducement she hoped would sway Mikhail. He had liked the strawberry graphic design for the Amoteh bathing suits, but he wasn't budging easily on letting anyone else take over the Bella project.

She sensed that Mikhail was enjoying himself in a very private game of his own making. He wasn't making her uncomfortable, and all the business dealings were flowing along nicely—except one, his insistence that she remain that first summer and personally handle the Bella Shop.

She had reluctantly agreed. Though she was certain she could eventually persuade Mikhail to hire another manager, she had begun designing the layout of the shop. One day of being reverted to a child by her parents and being called "Precious Blossom" in front of Mikhail—a man she wanted to influence—was enough to stretch any woman's nerves taut.

The name tossed her back into her carefree, happy childhood, not exactly the mental place for a determined, seasoned businesswoman facing a hard customer.

The humming sensation within her body had nothing to do with business, and she didn't want to think about the reason, who loomed just in front of her as she rounded the atrium's corner. With the sprawling indoor pool behind him, Jarek was hefting boards from a stack and carrying them to one side of the tile floor.

In a T-shirt and jeans and workman's boots, he was beautiful, the carpenter's tool belt slung around his hips. The bright day in the windows behind him framed every powerful line and gleamed on that wonderful, tanned skin.

In her mind, once more she felt those muscles slide around her, the nudge of his bicep against her breast. That rough callused hand had cupped her breast so gently, massaged until—

Jarek glanced at her, then his eyes ripped down her body and back up to her flushed face. His expression darkened as if he didn't like what he saw.

Leigh forced herself not to tremble again. The plain white business blouse with her minimizer bra beneath it, the black lined vest and skirt were perfect for work. Jarek was a man of moods so strong that they wrapped around her, but she didn't understand him. *She did understand the obvious shape of his desire last night—he had been aroused, and he had wanted her right then in the most primitive of ways—to stake his claim, his possession of her.*

That shocking understanding slammed into her. *Jarek not only wanted that passionate moment with her, he wanted more.* A man like Jarek would want everything, wide-open and undenied.

Wide-open and undenied. Hadn't she wanted the same? Hadn't she held her sweatshirt down with her fists to prevent herself from tearing it away and going for all that his kisses, that her aroused body ached for?

The coffee Leigh had been carrying in her other hand sloshed and a drop spilled to the floor as a jolt of sheer lust shot through her. In the mere feet separating them, she could actually sense him tense and heat. "I suppose you're the workman Mikhail said I'm to work with, right?"

He nodded, studying her in the afternoon light. "Do you have a problem with that?"

Problem? Problem? Leigh tried to focus on her sketched layout of the shop when she couldn't stop looking into those dark sea-green eyes. Jarek took the clipboard from her and began studying it, just as her parents wandered into the atrium.

Just the sight of them, mixed with the uncertain emotions Jarek had caused, was enough to make Leigh feel guilty—she should want them with her, but past experience said that Ed and Bliss could derail a business transaction without trying. Not that they would—they were sweet-looking, a little worn, but with that "together forever" look that always caught Leigh. Bliss's loose, flowing skirt and blouse seemed to match Ed's faded shirt, his khaki pants, and their socks and sandals were exactly alike. Her parents were huggable, soft and worn, and her heart softened every time she looked at them. She placed the coffee aside, because she knew they always hugged her. Both of them. At the same time. Ed and Bliss loved group hugs.

"Oh, Precious Blossom, we've been looking for you," Bliss called, coming to hug Leigh. "Group hug. All together now," Bliss said, smiling at Jarek. "You, too. You look as if you need a hug."

Jarek's expression didn't change, but Leigh noted that tiny curve to his mouth that said he was enjoying himself. He moved close to her, and for just a heartbeat, his hand cruised her waist and hip lightly. The way he looked down at her said he remembered last night, too, and desire still simmered, unfed within him.

Leigh hugged briefly and then eased away. She wasn't certain of herself, or of him, as Bliss exclaimed happily, "Ed and I are going to move into a house Jarek found for us. I'm going to have a goat, Precious! I've always wanted a goat. It's a kid, really, so she can't be milked for a while, but—"

The soft, huggable emotion enfolding Leigh dropped to the beautiful, but cold tile floor. She struggled to recover. Her parents had never lived in an actual house.

"A house Jarek found for you?" She turned to see Jarek's mild, too-innocent smile. "You're just one surprise after another, aren't you?"

"Everyone should have a surprise now and then, don't you think?" he asked too easily, and she knew he referred to last night.

Bliss tilted her head and thoughtfully smoothed the beads over her flowing dress. "You know, Precious, you have started the oddest habit of repeating everything anyone says."

Jarek seemed to be standing too close, and Leigh moved cautiously away. She couldn't combat reality, her parents in a house and Jarek, all at the same time. And her mother was very good at sensing auras. Leigh's were in turmoil; she didn't want Bliss to be upset.

"It's my parents' first home and it's small, dry, empty and in good shape," he said. "Ed and Bliss are welcome to—"

Leigh quickly calculated all the medical bills—and the bill for the damage to the hotel that her parents had just left—and subtracted that from her dwindling bank account. She would soon have to start making payments on the money she had borrowed. "Summer cottages are expensive, aren't they? I don't know that we can afford—"

Bliss hugged her again. "Oh, Precious, everything will be fine. I'm going to sell my tie-dye shirts and Ed is going to make beads and we'll sell them to the tourists. We'll open a stall on the pier and call it, 'Go With The Flow.' We'll be fine. We always are. You worry so. You really should use that worry stone that Ed made for you. It would relieve your stress, which is much, much too high. You didn't hear a word I said this morning. You seemed in another world."

"I have a lot on my mind," Leigh managed, the echoes of the San Francisco hotel manager's yelling still fresh in her mind. Ed had opened the balcony doors and had fed the pigeons on the carpet, and in return they left little gifts typical of well-fed birds. It had taken every bit of Leigh's considerable bargaining power to influence the manager not to press charges. But then, she'd been bargaining on her family's behalf for most of her life. Whatever the bargain, however cheap, her parents just could not live in a Stepanov home—or the complication of problems would ruin any business progress she'd made.

Leigh tried for an appealing alternative. "You've never lived in a house, Bliss. There are things to take care of."

Her mother waved her hand airily. "How much different can it be from a hotel, or the van? It has a bathroom and a shower, just like a campground. We're going to walk over there now and absorb its aura. I'll bet it's just filled with love. Only love could create sons as sweet and thoughtful as Jarek and Mikhail. The van is being difficult, but Jarek said he'd drive it over later. We can start moving in then. Do you want to come with us, Precious Blossom? Oh, I wish you hadn't changed your name. Your birth name suits you so well."

Ed rubbed his worn headband, his favorite, and Leigh mourned the new lines etched on his face. The man who had once carried her on his shoulders, who had been so strong, now was gaunt, and his shoulders slumped. His bald spot was larger, his hair thinner and gray within its scraggly ponytail.

He smiled at Leigh. "Sometimes I wish we could go back to those days when you ran around without a stitch, and without a worry, too. Your mother is right. You really should use your worry stone. Where is it, anyway? I haven't seen it."

"I've been afraid I would lose it. It's in my room. I'll use it, I promise." A jolt of pure, undiluted guilt hit Leigh. She felt six years old again and caught in some wrongdoing. When she had started her first job with benefits and was struggling to balance her life, and theirs, Ed had worked very hard to fashion the worry stone from obsidian, a stress-reliever. It now lay in a forgotten corner of her luggage.

Ed beamed at her. "I love you, Precious. Peace."

"Blessings, Ed," she returned, loving him.

Leigh found Jarek, who hadn't seemed to hear the conversation, as he flipped on the power saw and it ripped across a board. The whine grated against her rising temper. Once more, Jarek had interfered in her life; she was losing control—of her life and of her work and of—

When her parents were gone, she walked to tap him on the shoulder and the saw stopped. Jarek lifted his safety glasses to the top of his head, and the green of his eyes was as cool as seagrass. Towering over her, he looked just as immovable as his brother, and more—just more, Leigh decided. Jarek was a concentrated package with all sorts of danger zones, moody little edges that could shift from brooding into playful before she could change the venue. She had to handle him—she flipped over that thought—she had already handled him, touched him, *felt him.*

She had to place all those images and sensations humming in her body aside. She had to influence him to change the offer of the house. "I want to talk with you."

"Talk."

The single word cut across the atrium. Jarek's legs were

braced apart on the tile floor, his arms crossed in front of him. A muscle contracted in that taut jaw, and the mouth that had heated and sensitized hers was set into a grim line; the pirate was preparing for battle.

Jarek loved to watch Leigh's expressions—that slight frown, that little sensual curl at her mouth's right corner and then that pursing of her lips as she prepared her thoughts.

"It won't be so bad," he offered, just to help her get started. His body still ached from last night, the lack of sleep gnawing at him. For just a moment, he'd sensed that Leigh might throw away all caution and come to him, love him as wildly as he desired, but then she'd withdrawn into her control once more.

But then, what would they each have in taking each other that quickly? he wondered darkly. More? Or less? Bodies and souls could be locked in a struggle against each other. Was he ready to place Annabelle's memory totally aside?

He didn't know anything but one truth—he wanted Leigh, desired her, ached for her.

Leigh tapped her pen on her clipboard and narrowed her eyes, considering him. She was a very passionate woman, taking her time in getting revved up. She was circling the problem, weighing the bargaining points and lining up the delivery. "It's bad," she answered. "I've got all of my problems in one locale. Except for my brother. He'll probably turn up now that Ed and Bliss are here. He knows that I can't refuse him anything when they ask me to help. But the biggest problem is standing in front of me."

"How's Morris?" he asked, brooding over that bouquet Mikhail had said was sent to Leigh. Did she talk to Morris last night? Would dear Morris turn up to share her room, for supposed business purposes?

Jarek didn't like the dark, brooding jealousy that had wrapped itself around him. Yet it was there, nettling and nudging. He'd held Leigh in his arms, kissed her, and he didn't want Morris or any other man experiencing those exciting, exquisite purrs, or the way her body quaked and heated.

She looked at him blankly. "Morris? Morris is always fine. Has he called here?"

Then slowly Leigh frowned. "You think that I got where I am by sleeping with the boss, don't you? It's not a new idea, you know. I'm younger than he is. I came up the Bella ladder fast. We work together all the time. We travel together. Some people put two and two together and get five. I might expect that from you. But Morris is my mentor and friend, nothing more."

"What do you mean, 'expect' that from me?"

She waved her hand airily. "You're very physical... basic...elemental. Morris is more...mental. It's only natural that your ideas are based in the physical. I saw last night how you—"

Jarek wasn't exactly happy about the previous night; he'd spent it with a certain very distinguishable ache and the knowledge that life—in the form of one "Precious Blossom"—had come to jerk him out of mourning whether he liked it or not. His instincts told him to take care of Leigh, to share her life and her bed. His mind said he hadn't come completely free of the past.

On the other hand, because he had that Stepanov pride and perhaps—if he admitted the truth—a little arrogance, he needed her to do a bit of long-term wanting, too. "It's logical that your parents are near you, you know. You can check on them easily."

Leigh picked up her coffee and sipped it, clearly thinking about how she was going to manage everything. "What's this about a goat?"

"We saw a herd of them on the way up from California. Bliss said she'd always wanted a goat and a garden, but that they'd never stayed long enough in one place. I bought a kid for her. The kid's name is now Lovely Lotus."

Leigh sat in a chaise lounge by the pool, then leaned back, her hand over her eyes. "A female. That means—"

Jarek enjoyed the view of feminine curves, then lifted her feet up and took the coffee from her. "Right. More kids. That's how it works generally."

Leigh groaned once and again. "Goats. Fences. People complaining about them eating things other than grass—maybe clothes. Food bills. Vet bills. They hid a dying buffalo once and you have no idea how much that cost, and the fine for transporting and stealing protected wildlife."

She lifted the hand over her eyes and glared at him. "Goats aren't exactly welcome in most rental situations, you know. Your parents might not like one in their rental house. I *know* that any hotels or condos I might get my parents into won't like them."

"It did okay in the resort last night. There wasn't much to munch on in the bathroom after it ate the soap. We forgot to remove that. I took her over to Dad's workshop early this morning. He's enjoying her. He tended goats in the old country."

Leigh's painful groan, the way her hand flopped over her face, said she was waiting for Mikhail's eviction notice and the cancellation of any hopes for a Bella shop.

Jarek sat on his haunches at her side and couldn't help smiling. He rubbed the top of her head playfully. "You need to relax, Precious."

The name suited her, he decided, considering her pink lips, and remembering the tropical heat within them.

She groaned again, and turned her head slowly to look at him. Jarek's heart almost stopped as he looked at her.

"Do you think I have any chance of getting Mikhail to let someone else handle the development of this project? Any chance at all?" she asked desperately.

He eased his finger through an enticing curl. Leigh's hair caught the sun and seemed to burn in his hand, gold and fiery silk dragged along his darker skin, the image erotic and tantalizing. "Not one. Looks like you're set for the summer. You might as well enjoy it."

Leigh suddenly reached out to push him back, and unbalanced, Jarek sat on the floor. She launched to her feet and stood over him, hands on her waist.

The view was enticing, her blouse gaping just that bit, tight around her breasts, her legs smooth and slender and long just beside him.

"Please don't hurt me," Jarek teased quietly, though excitement charged through him as he wondered what she would do next.

"I'd like to toss you into that pool, but you're too big."

"You're not," he said as he came to his feet, more alive than he had been in years. Jarek lifted Leigh and tossed her into the pool.

She came up sputtering, her shoes floating by her side. She snatched each one and grimly made her way to the steps. While she surged out of the water, those gold eyes burned and lashed at him angrily. Her hair waved in strands along her cheek, water spiked her lashes and beaded her face. Her damp clothes clung to every curve, and Jarek knew the emotion stirring in him at that moment could only be defined as lust.

But then there was the other softer emotion that caused his chest to ache, as if his heart had just opened to a new beginning without quite leaving the past. As if it were uncertain, fearing—Jarek scowled at Leigh. He wasn't certain he liked the sensation of being emotional or vulnerable, not at his age.

Always prowling his domain, aware of any riffles in the well-ordered halls, Mikhail came to stand beside Jarek. "Problems, Leigh?"

"None that I can't handle. Thank you," she returned grimly and stalked past Jarek, her eyes still blazing at him.

As the brothers watched Leigh squish her way out of the atrium, Mikhail said, "Ed and Bliss really appreciate the folks' old home. So do I. They need to leave the Amoteh. There are already problems with the staff. For one thing they're vegetarians. Georgia didn't like the lecture on being carnivorous and eating meat.''

Jarek watched the sway of Leigh's hips and realized uncomfortably that his body had responded to hers. Every instinct told him to go after her, kiss her, and make love to her until they were both exhausted—then start all over again.

That taut, brooding, hunger remained with Jarek for the rest of the evening. After filling the van with groceries, he drove it to the cottage by the shore. It sputtered and died as if it were home and wasn't finding another highway.

His mother had already come to visit, and the Stepanovs' discarded odd assortment of furniture was appreciated by Ed and Bliss. When Jarek had finished helping them unpack the van and had declined their offer of veggie burgers for dinner, Ed and Bliss stood, hand in hand, smiling at him. ''Precious has a beautiful heart, you know,'' Bliss said quietly. ''She's been racing too hard through life, working too hard and not taking time for herself, but she's a giving, loving girl. You won't break her heart, will you?''

''No, I won't,'' Jarek said and wondered how Bliss sensed the uncertain emotions he had for Leigh.

''Her aura when she stood beside you today was simply— throbbing, yes, I guess that's a good word. Or pulsing and alive with warmth. She's upset, and not about work, either. You disturb her. She doesn't know what to do about you. Precious gets upset when things can't be explained or orderly, or she doesn't know how she feels. That's why surprises upset her so.''

Life had also handed him a surprise—Leigh. ''If it helps, I don't know what to do about her, either.''

''So then, everything will be just fine,'' Ed said firmly with a smile. ''Go with the flow, man. Peace and blessings.''

When Jarek walked down the hillside toward Amoteh, he turned to see Ed and Bliss, framed by the dying sun as they sat on a blanket, lotus-style, the kid sprawled between them, wearing a flower garland. With the little white cottage and picket fence behind them, they looked as if they belonged.

Where did he belong? Jarek wondered as he studied the sun skimming the ocean swells and the whites of the gulls' wings.

How long ago had he tossed his wedding ring into the ocean and cursed life for leaving him without his wife? He had thrown Chief Kamakani's curse back at him. Did he belong in the past with Annabelle's memory?

Or in the stormy excitement, the stirring of his blood and senses and heart that was Leigh?

Leigh wiped the sweat from her face with a towel and turned up the speed on the Amoteh's treadmill. As a representative of a sportswear company, she wanted a healthy, well-toned body.

The exercise room overlooked the shoreline with the setting sun skimming the Pacific's swells, the waves frothing at the brown sand. She had a clear view of the solitary man facing toward Deadman's Rock and Strawberry Hill. Leigh had heard of "survivor's guilt." Did Jarek miss his wife so much that he couldn't release his guilt for living when she had died?

Leigh checked her vital signs and knew that no amount of exercise was going to wipe Jarek from her mind, or her body.

She slowed, then turned off the machine and walked to the massive windows overlooking the shore. She placed her hand against the glass still warm from the sun and shook her head. Leigh couldn't afford Jarek, he could unbalance the world she'd built so carefully.

She took the Bella headband from her head and gripped it in her fist. Ed and Bliss loved Jarek. But then they would. They loved everyone, and the small cottage had endeared him to them.

For the moment, they were safe and warm and happy. Fadey hadn't wanted the rental check she delivered to the Stepanov Furniture shop. "You upset me, little girl. Come, kiss my cheek and go see your parents. My wife says they are special and need a little help now. You think that I am so hungry for money that I would take your money? You come to the house when you can and do not let Mikhail work you so hard. He loves work too much, I think, after his wife left him. Maybe before. He wanted to give the people here employment, but she wanted the city—no small town for her, and no babies either.''

Fadey had sighed mournfully and smoothed oil onto a walnut table. He rubbed it with a rag and wishes. "I will die without grandbabies to hold on my knee. No grandsons to carry on the Stepanov name here. No granddaughters to cuddle and kiss and babysit. I have no little girls to teach the *chaepitie,* the tea ceremony. When my hands and my wife's begin to shake and we cannot prepare the *samovar* for tea, what little girl will know how to serve properly? Oh, my sons do, but to see a woman—tea making is so graceful in a woman's hands—not a man's big, rough ones.''

Then he'd looked at her with those clear gray eyes. "I have two good, healthy sons. You take one, please. I like you. You would make grandbabies for Fadey, wouldn't you? Because you love so deeply, you deserve a baby of your own. That woman of Mikhail's, she killed his baby...and maybe his heart, too. Jarek's wife wasn't strong in her heart. She felt it made her less than a woman not to have children. So sad, she was—little Annabelle. Some people say the Hawaiian's curse took her, because Jarek loved her so much. Some people think she went there that day to dance in front of the chief's grave, to stop his curse so that her babies would live.''

Now, Leigh looked at Jarek, small when placed against the magnificence of the ocean. Whatever was happening between them, she sensed that he still mourned his wife and hadn't let her go. Leigh knew bargaining and business and survival. But somewhere along the way, she had missed the essentials of being a woman and enjoying life. Maybe Annabelle knew that life was about being a woman and loving enough to risk having a baby for the man she loved.

Leigh wasn't certain she could love a man that deeply. Her life was focused on survival, not dreams for herself. Because she was driven? Yes, but also because she wanted the best for her family.

That left little time for her own needs, and Jarek had presented problems she hadn't expected—like the need to touch him, to smooth her hands over his skin, that rough texture exciting her hands, those sea-green eyes darkening as he looked at her.

"Leave me alone, Jarek," she whispered, even as she hungered to see him again.

Five

Jarek noted the small light moving on the pathway from the Amoteh Resort to Ed and Bliss's cottage.

At eleven o'clock at night, Jarek prowled the night. Uneasy with the silence of his house, the memory of Leigh igniting, he had walked out onto the tourist pier, listening to the incoming tide, the familiar creaks and the gentle-sounding bumps that told of rental boats, moored to other nearby piers. The familiar sound and scents he'd known all his life circled him, but they had changed.

He had changed. Leigh's body flowing against his, those feminine, little hungry purrs and that soft skin beneath his cruising hand had told him that he was very much alive.

Jarek inhaled the salt air and studied the stars he knew so well; in his grief for Annabelle, he'd set off sailing by the stars, pitting himself against his grief and his guilt.

But he'd lived and struggled with his conscience and life had gone on. During the day, tourists flowed in and out of the shops, taking Lannie's excursion sightseeing boat, eating chowders, sourdough bread and hot dogs, and buying sea-shells, neatly packaged and shipped from China. Jarek had grown up here, hauling Dungeness crabs to Norris at the Crab Shack, catching and preparing bait for those who wanted ocean fishing—the scent of the past mixed with the salt air.

He noted Lars Anders's trawler sliding through the ocean night, ignoring the Coast Guard regulations for clear display of running lights. He'd been convicted of a few minor crimes, and had paid heavy fines for carelessly tearing apart oyster beds farther north.

A brawling bully, Lars didn't like the Stepanovs. Years ago, his abused wife and son had sought shelter in the Stepanov home. When Lars came to retrieve her and threatened the Stepanovs, he met Fadey's big fist—after Stepanov's solid slap had insulted him more in front of his wife.

She had long ago reached safety and a new life, but Lars hadn't forgotten. After a brawl with Mikhail and one with Jarek, he still brooded about revenge. A regular at the Sea-gull's Perch, he was often drunk and ugly and incensed that Mikhail's "classy, high-dollar, overcharging resort" wouldn't let him deliver oysters and other seafood directly. During tour-ist season, Lars made a hefty living and because of his less than high ethics, had been banned from the Amoteh.

Jarek frowned, noting the unlit house on the hill. Ed and Bliss were probably now sleeping, exhausted from their trip. But another flash of light near the house caused him to be suspicious. Lars and his crew were in port and gossip would soon point to the potential easy victims.

Jarek moved quickly up the sandy path toward the cottage nestled on the edge of the wind-deformed pines. As he came close, the moonlight slid over the small house, the white picket fence. A soft flash of light drew him to the scraggy, windswept pine and the old, rusted van. The hood was open and someone was lifting the light over the motor.

The dim glow revealed Leigh's intent face and Jarek stopped to admire the way her hips curved, the length of her legs in the sweatpants as she stood on tiptoe. Apparently experienced at what she was doing, Leigh hung the flashlight from the hood, aiming it down into the motor. She bent to pick up a small toolbox and placed it on the rusted, dented fender, inspecting the jumbled contents.

Jarek couldn't resist. He came closer, leaned against the fender and handed her a wrench when she next straightened. "Thanks," she said in a distracted tone as she bent once again into the motor.

"Anytime," he answered, admiring the rounded line of her backside.

He waited while she stiffened and slowly lifted her head out of the motor. She frowned at him. "Go away. I'm busy."

"I see that."

"I know about motors. I've played mechanic for as long as I can remember. While I might want a rental company to fix the car they gave me, as a point in good business practice, I can manage my parents' van."

He peered down into the motor. "Any special reason why you want to remove the distributor cap at this hour?"

Leigh neatly removed the cap, eased the hood closed and placed the cap in the tool box. She opened the van's rear door and slid the box into it. "Don't you fix it for them. I don't want them going anywhere. At least, not until I can find a place away from here."

"What's wrong with here?"

"Too many problems."

"They seem happy enough here."

Leigh sighed deeply. "That can change. Believe me, I've had experience. You didn't do anyone any favors by bringing them here. I could have managed—"

"Could you?" The wind played in her hair and Jarek reached out to smooth it, his touch lingering in the silky strands.

The moonlight danced across her lashes as she tilted her head and studied him. "You miss her, don't you? Your wife?"

There it was, he thought, the softness and the caring woman. Leigh wouldn't want to hear now that she looked and sounded so much like Bliss. "Sometimes. Sometimes I think it was all a dream. Sometimes I think I hear her cry out to me in the squalls, like the mythical Lorelei who called sailors to their deaths."

Jarek didn't want to think about the nightmare of seeing Annabelle lying pale and lifeless in that bed of seaweed.

"You shouldn't blame yourself. I've heard the stories. They're all the same. Your wife was experienced with the small motorboat. Maybe she needed time alone—women do, sometimes."

That day flashed back at Jarek. "We had argued. She wanted to dance in front of the chief's grave and remove the curse—she believed Kamakani's curse that ill would befall those on the shore here, because he couldn't return to his homeland. He died up on Strawberry Hill—we played there as children, and Annabelle had become obsessed with that curse. Her boat came back. She didn't. Not for a time—then they called me to come identify her."

"I understand that passage across the inlet isn't usually dangerous. On the ocean side, yes—where the force of the swells could propel a boat against the rock." Leigh lifted her hair and the night wind rummaged through her curls until they looked like sea froth touched by moonlight.

Jarek thought of how many times he'd sat in that same boat, during the same time Annabelle would have passed Deadman's Rock. The water had carried him safely away. Could Annabelle have wanted to kill herself that day? Could she possibly have taken the outer course, the dangerous ocean side of Deadman's Rock? Maybe the ancient Hawaiian's curse was true, because she was gone and his guilt remained.

It only seemed natural to take Leigh's hand, to protect her in the night. "I'll walk you back."

The slight tensing of that small hand in his told him that Leigh was unfamiliar with sharing herself. Then her fingers relaxed, her palm so soft against his, the fingers delicate in his broad, callused workman's hand.

The wind caught her curls, tossing them, and he wondered distantly, briefly, if Kamakani toyed with the idea of claiming her, too.

"I'm worried about my parents, Jarek. I don't know if they can change now, at their age, and settle down."

As the moonlight painted a silver edge over her profile, he wondered if she ever worried about herself. "Give them time."

"I've got to go. I'm exhausted and that's not the time to be around you."

Now *that* tidbit interested Jarek and jarred him back from the past. Everything about Leigh interested him. He held her hand when she would have moved away, and brought it to his lips. "Why not?"

Leigh turned to him and firmly tugged her hand free. "Because you're you. Playful, boyish, flirtatious, moody. One moment you're arrogant, the next you— I don't have time for any of that. I like the predictable, and you're not. I understand that if there's a storm and someone needing help, you're the first to hop in a boat and sail into a storm. You're a favorite at the Seagull, and sometimes you even tend bar there. There's a brooding, bad boy element in you that draws women. You come to the dances and dinners at the Amoteh, though I can't imagine you all dressed up. Arm-wrestling matches, bets on whatever, and today, I heard one of the maids discussing how Marcella tried to—to have you on the very bed that I—that you—you know, the showroom bed."

Marcella's attempted seduction had disgusted him. With the excuse that she wanted to know more about the furniture, she'd met him in the showroom. Marcella's overlarge breast implants, her carefully pampered body hadn't appealed as she stripped for him, blocking the doorway. Jarek had simply opened the showroom window and had stepped out into the fresh salt air away from her too-heavy scent.

Jarek didn't like the picture Leigh had painted of him. He worked hard and he filled his life. He tried to escape the nightmare of Annabelle and the nagging guilt that always found him.

He tore thoughts of Annabelle from him and studied Leigh. "Our bed, you mean? The one we shared?"

"I don't like to think of it that way, and I was speaking clinically—explaining the reasons I'd prefer to stay away from you. You're taking my appraisal personally and that isn't how it is intended. I'm simply pointing out the whys. I was exhausted and frustrated and upset last night and that's why—"

"Why you turned to fire in my arms? Is that what you were going to say? You see me as a playboy, right? How am I supposed to take that? I'm thirty-six, Leigh, and I'm responsible for my actions."

He saw no reason to explain the loneliness that drew him to the Seagull, nor his brother's good-natured bullying to appear at Amoteh dances.

"Bliss says you're a passionate man. That you live life to the fullest. What I see and hear about is a man who breaks women's hearts, toying with them without any intention of following up his flirtations. As I said, I don't have time for games."

Her appraisal nettled and before he could stop himself, Jarek had tugged her into his arms. "Do you have time for this?" he asked before taking her mouth hungrily.

There it was, the fire and the hunger warming her lips, the softness of her body as she responded, flowing against him.

There it was, the greed in the grasp of her fingers in his hair, the parting of her lips.

There it was, his tenderness and desire for a woman who thought little of him.

He eased slowly away and Leigh leaned slightly toward him before she caught her balance. She licked her lips slowly and the surge of desire locked within him. For just a heartbeat, he'd sensed the awakening within her, the prowling, passionate woman.

"You're very experienced," she whispered unevenly, her fists tight at her side. "I'd better go."

Jarek watched her move up the steps of the Amoteh, his instincts telling him to go after her. His "experience" ran to a few young necking parties and marital intimacies with his wife. What Leigh had tasted, what he had given her, was his need for her, a tenderness that lay beneath his obvious desire.

He slashed his hand over his face and listened to his heart pounding more quickly than the sound of the waves frothing at the shoreline. He'd charted a hard course with a woman who thought little of him, and it seemed that he had little to say about it. Where was his pride? he wondered. Where was his grief or anything that usually found him brooding and roaming the night?

Only his fascination for Leigh remained, a poor sorry thing when she thought little of him.

Jarek found himself smiling at the moon. He almost pitied himself for what he would suffer when she discovered how else he had interfered with her life—with his "interference," her brother would arrive soon, and Ryan wasn't an easy customer.

But having Leigh's family all in one place meant she wasn't likely to be running after them and even more exhausted. If crises happened, Jarek and his family would help.

Then because Jarek had to and didn't want to explain the need, he raised his face to the wind and freed the long, lonely howl lurking in him.

Outlined at the top of the steps for just a moment, Leigh stopped and turned slowly. Jarek blew her a flamboyant kiss, and then she turned to run the rest of the way, disappearing into the Amoteh.

The shadow moving in the dark turned out to be Ed, clad in a long gown. "Hey, man. That howling was cool. Sort of a cleansing, huh? I feel like that sometimes myself when Precious gets all stewed up and starts lecturing Bliss and me. She means well, though, and she loves us. Nice night, huh? Bliss said your soul was hungry and grieving and didn't know what to make of Precious, but that she filled something inside you. You just have to take her as she is, man. Sweet, lovable, a little too old for her age. She worries too much, always has. Come in and I'll play my flute for you. It's calming."

"Thanks, that would be nice." Jarek could use soothing after Leigh's bruising assessment of him.

But "soothing" wasn't how he felt later, lying in his bed alone, his body still humming with desire for Leigh.

There was another hunger, too, that he wasn't quite ready to accept.

The next morning, Leigh tried once more to persuade Mikhail to let someone else take over running the shop. She failed. For some reason the eldest Stepanov brother seemed to be very accommodating, except for that one issue—no one else would manage the shop. A phone call to her parents found Bliss excited about the garden she was planning. Ed had found that the van wouldn't start, but he wasn't concerned.

Leigh shivered as she remembered the long, lonely howl that could only have come from Jarek. *What kind of a man would do such a thing?*

She glanced at him across a stack of boxes packed with Bella Swimwear and covered with sawdust.

A storm of sawdust swirled around Jarek. He stood at the power saw, legs braced as he guided the boards through his markings. The sawdust caught on his gleaming bare skin, covered those sliding muscles of his back and chest and arms and—that taut backside and long powerful legs. An emotion zapped her and she could only uneasily define it as lust.

Leigh studied him from over her clipboard. Today, humming as he worked intently, efficiently, safety glasses over his eyes, he seemed innocent enough.

She braced herself. He was Mikhail's brother, after all. It

wouldn't do to have Mikhail upset. She could put everything into a business perspective and manage a working relationship with Jarek. Leigh had managed uncomfortable situations before where personalities and work didn't mix well. She could manage, she thought again as she braced herself for a pleasant, but firm meeting with Jarek. "Is everything going according to the plans? Any problems?" she asked in what she hoped was a businesslike, but pleasant tone.

He shook his head and continued guiding a board through the ripping saw. When she moved closer, braced to establish a firm, but pleasant working relationship, Jarek glanced down at her. "Stand back," he ordered sharply.

His tone surprised her, and Leigh stepped back, her heel catching on a heavy power cord. Unbalanced, she began to fall, and Jarek turned suddenly, flipped off the power saw and reached for her.

He'd moved so quickly, startling her. His hands held her upper arms firmly as she looked up at him. "How clumsy of me. Thank you."

"You're very welcome. Stay out of my way, okay?" He grinned with enough impact to take her breath away. Her heart felt like dancing, her skin like it had been touched by rain and summer sunlight, and somewhere deep inside her, she felt carefree and young.

"Um…when do you think the shop will be done? I mean I ordered the display racks and Mikhail has said that he wants the shop in tip-top running order right away. It's already June and we should be open already. Do you think—"

"He told me. Dad and Mikhail and I are finishing it tonight."

"Oh. I'm sorry that it's taking your family away from their furniture business."

Jarek lifted the safety glasses over his head and studied her. "What's this all about? This chitchat? What do you want?"

His blunt questions hit her, pinned her to what she did want—to kiss him. He looked delicious in sweat and sawdust and she shivered as an image of all that bare body next to hers— "Nothing, absolutely nothing. I'm trying to get along with you, that's all."

His eyes narrowed. "You're making nice? You don't want to lose that big fat contract and bonus? Let me relieve your mind. I don't have anything to do with Mikhail's business contracts. I like working with wood. If you don't have anything else to say to me, please stay back where it's safe."

Leigh wasn't used to being ordered and it was *her* project. *Her* bonus. Jarek's mood was out of place in a business arrangement. "You're temperamental this morning. You're growling."

"I had a hard night." Jarek's well-muscled arms crossed in front of him and he locked his boots on the sawdust-covered floor. "Some woman kissed me out in the moonlight last night. It was a kiss that I couldn't toss away. I took it to bed with me, and there it stayed, hot and ready. What about you? Sleep well?"

From his stance, she knew he was set to argue. So was she. She'd had dreams of him as her lover in that big sprawling showroom bed. "I would have thought that howl would have released some tension."

"Not when you're around." Jarek glanced at the young maid walking toward him and his hard expression softened. The petite, leggy blonde's uniform was unbuttoned down to the crevice of her breasts.

She handed him a large glass of lemonade and Jarek said, "Hi, Louise. Mmm, that looks good. Thanks."

Leigh noted darkly how the girl stood close to him, smoothing his arms and batting her lashes. "Anytime, Jarek," she crooned.

He watched her swaying walk away from him and then lifted the glass of lemonade and drank it thirstily. He handed the empty glass to Leigh and even with the icy drink chilling his lips, his light kiss tasted of a stormy heat.

PLAY LUCKY 7
and get
FREE Gifts!

HOW TO PLAY:

1. With a coin, carefully scratch off the gold area at the right. Then check the claim chart to see what we have for you — **2 FREE BOOKS** and a **FREE GIFT** — **ALL YOURS FREE!**

2. Send back the card and you'll receive two brand-new Silhouette Desire® novels. These books have a cover price of $3.99 each in the U.S. and $4.50 each in Canada, but they are yours to keep absolutely free.

3. There's no catch. You're under no obligation to buy anything. We charge nothing — **ZERO** — for your first shipment. And you don't have to make any minimum number of purchases — not even one!

4. The fact is, thousands of readers enjoy receiving books by mail from the Silhouette Reader Service®. They enjoy the convenience of home delivery...they like getting the best new novels at discount prices, BEFORE they're available in stores...and they love their *Heart to Heart* subscriber newsletter featuring author news, horoscopes, recipes, book reviews and much more!

5. We hope that after receiving your free books you'll want to remain a subscriber. But the choice is yours — to continue or cancel, any time at all! So why not take us up on our invitation, with no risk of any kind. You'll be glad you did!

We can't tell you what it is...but we're sure you'll like it! A surprise **FREE GIFT** just for playing LUCKY 7!

NO COST! NO OBLIGATION TO BUY!

NO PURCHASE NECESSARY!

Scratch off the gold area with a coin.
Then check below to
see the gifts you get!

326 SDL DNKR   225 SDL DNKL

FIRST NAME	LAST NAME

ADDRESS

APT.#	CITY

STATE/PROV.   ZIP/POSTAL CODE   (S-D-04/02)

Worth **2 FREE BOOKS** plus a **FREE GIFT!**

Worth **2 FREE BOOKS!**

Worth **1 FREE BOOK!**

Try Again!

The Silhouette Reader Service® — Here's how it works:

Accepting your 2 free books and gift places you under no obligation to buy anything. You may keep the books and gift and return the shipping statement marked "cancel." If you do not cancel, about a month later we'll send you 6 additional books and bill you just $3.34 each in the U.S., or $3.74 each in Canada, plus 25¢ shipping & handling per book and applicable taxes if any.* That's the complete price and — compared to cover prices of $3.99 each in the U.S. and $4.50 each in Canada — it's quite a bargain! You may cancel at any time, but if you choose to continue, every month we'll send you 6 more books, which you may either purchase at the discount price or return to us and cancel your subscription.

*Terms and prices subject to change without notice. Sales tax applicable in N.Y. Canadian residents will be charged applicable provincial taxes and GST.

If offer card is missing write to: Silhouette Reader Service, 3010 Walden Ave., P.O. Box 1867, Buffalo NY 14240-1867

BUSINESS REPLY MAIL

FIRST-CLASS MAIL   PERMIT NO. 717-003   BUFFALO, NY

POSTAGE WILL BE PAID BY ADDRESSEE

SILHOUETTE READER SERVICE
3010 WALDEN AVE
PO BOX 1867
BUFFALO NY 14240-9952

NO POSTAGE
NECESSARY
IF MAILED
IN THE
UNITED STATES

Jarek smiled at her and brushed her hair. "Sawdust. You look good in it. And that hot jealous look."

"Me? I've never been jealous in my life." But Jarek's look said he'd caught that unfamiliar, startling angry vibration as Louise had flirted with him.

"I told you, I loved my wife. I blame myself for her death, but I don't need just any woman's body to enjoy living. And I've known Louise since she was born. It seems that I prefer a woman whose hair tosses in the wind like coppery sea froth, whose eyes change from the shade of dark honey to that of light gold, and whose kisses tell me she feels the same, no matter what words she gives me."

He nodded, tugged down his safety glasses and returned to work, the sun gleaming through the windows catching the almost graceful movements of power and experience. Leigh stood wrapped in the echo of his deep voice. *Whose hair tosses in the night wind like coppery sea froth, whose eyes change from the shade of dark honey to that of light gold, and whose kisses tell me she feels the same....*

Jarek was talking about her, about a deep stark emotion that she sensed he had shared with no one—his love of his wife, and his nagging guilt. The ring of truth frightened her, how it affected her, how much she ached for him. He'd spoken baldly to her, like a man would speak to a woman he loved. *Loved!* Her? Why her?

Leigh decided to hurry herself to safety and space where Jarek's words couldn't shatter her. "I'll...I'll just take this down to the kitchen."

She wished she hadn't bumped into the stack of unpacked boxes, and then on the rebound against a new wall. She flattened herself against it for just a moment while Jarek continued to work. The wall was safe and dependable. He wasn't.

In the kitchen, she found Mikhail sipping his coffee and reading a newspaper, feet propped on a chair, completely relaxed. It was disconcerting to see Mikhail relaxed. The Stepanov brothers were too potent and irritating and—and just once, she'd like to see someone really get to Mikhail, really tip his control.

He glanced at her, then a grin that reminded her of Jarek's warmed his face. "Playing in sawdust? How's it going?"

She placed the glass on the table. "Everything is going fine. Just fine," she stated grimly. "I understand you're helping complete the shop."

"I like to work with my hands. Physical work relieves stress and tension. You should relax a little, Leigh. From the plans I've seen, you're completely in control of a really good project."

"Thanks." She didn't feel like talking business, or pushing Mikhail for once. Because Jarek was occupying too much of her mind. She sat down to brood over the cherry pastry confection Georgia had just served her.

She was a fool for wanting to see Jarek again, but she did. "Thanks. I just work out in the evenings, Mikhail. I could help tonight—to get my exercise. Anything to get the shop up in stocking order, you know. I'll need time to get the displays just right."

"That would be very nice," he answered formally, and rose to his feet. She wondered why he whistled as he walked away, a surprise in the very stern businessman, Mr. Mikhail Stepanov.

That night, Leigh tried to seem confident as she approached the three tall Stepanov men already ripping through wood and pounding and yelling over the sound of the saw.

Jarek lowered the power nail driver when he saw her. He studied her T-shirt, sweatpants and pricey running shoes. He frowned at the red bandanna she'd found and had tied around her hair. "What's *she* doing here?"

Fadey grinned at her as she stepped through the unfinished wide doorway. He moved quickly, enclosing her with a bear hug and lifting her off her feet as he turned in a circle. He placed her on her feet. An expert at seeing how his father's bear hugs affected people, Mikhail put out a hand to brace her until she caught her balance.

"I came to help. Mikhail said I could," she told Jarek who was scowling at her.

"She's a girl," Jarek stated darkly. "She'll get in the way. She'll get hurt."

"Just tell me what to do. I can handle myself. And back off, buddy. I've worked construction before. How do you think I got my first business suit for a job interview?"

Fadey let out a whoop that ended in roaring laughter. Mikhail turned quickly, but she thought she saw him grin at Jarek, who was still scowling. He looked down, then up her taut body. "You could sweep and clean up, I guess. The shop vacuum is over there. Just stay out of the way. If you get hurt, we'll have to wait on you and you'll cost us time."

Leigh grabbed the nearest broom and started sweeping furiously. She wasn't leaving because of Jarek's taunts. She didn't understand his boyish grin at Mikhail and Fadey, or his chuckle.

For the next two hours, she sweated and carried nails and picked up blocks and swept and tried not to show how tired she was. Once, while she was carrying a supply of nails to Fadey who was hammering inside a dressing room, he looked down at her and grinned. "Not so bad, is it, little girl? This working together, not business all the time?"

She grinned back at him. "Yes, it's good...seeing something come to life like this."

"You're a good little girl." Then he picked her up and walked out of the closet.

Leigh couldn't help laughing. The happy carefree feeling just erupted and curled and warmed and came out in laughter.

"That's good," Fadey said quietly. "Good to laugh so open like that."

Then he tossed her into Jarek's waiting arms. "Here, you take the little one. She is tired. Maybe a walk along the shore. She needs some fresh air after doing business all day with

Mikhail. We're done for tonight anyway. Tomorrow night we panel. You order fast delivery tomorrow, little girl. Panels for the walls and dressing rooms. After that, it is small work. One-man work. Jarek can put up shelves and mirrors. You tell him where they go.''

But Leigh couldn't breathe, couldn't talk, because Jarek's tanned face was too close to hers. The texture spoke of sunlight and wind; the tension in his body told of his desire for her. His heart beat heavily beneath her hand, and those sea-green eyes were close, so close, the heat of his body burning hers, every finger of his hands imprinted upon her waist and her legs.

She couldn't resist smoothing away the sawdust that had caught in his eyebrows, dusting lightly that on his cheek. Then again, time seemed to hold still, swirling around them as if they were alone.

"Let me down," she whispered, aware that her breast rested against that muscled chest.

He nodded but held her still and close to him. In that instant, she could have thrown her arms around him and taken his mouth. But she couldn't risk Jarek.

There was just that closing of his expression, the hardening of his mouth that told her he understood.

He lowered her to stand in front of him, and Leigh quickly moved away. She glanced at Fadey who was beaming at her.

"Thank you so much, Fadey. I want this shop to be a success."

Fadey's powerful arms enclosed her and he lifted her off her feet again as he kissed one cheek and then the other. "You try too hard, little one," he whispered against her ear. "Relax. Enjoy life a little."

Over Fadey's shoulder, Jarek was studying her. "She doesn't know how," he said quietly.

"Ha. Then she will learn. She learns good," Fadey said as he released Leigh and turned to hug each of his sons. He placed his arm around Mikhail's shoulders and danced a play-ful little jig. "See you tomorrow. You, too, little girl."

With a nod, Mikhail went down the hallway toward his office, while Fadey slipped out the side door. Jarek unplugged the power saw and turned off the lights, and the moonlight coming through the windows kicked the pool's reflection up into his face. "How about that walk?"

Leigh shook her head, remembering her reaction to him the past two nights. First, shocking heat and hunger and then the understanding of his grief and his guilt, the softness for him unexpected, revealing a depth she hadn't considered.

When he held out that big square workman's hand to her, she found herself taking it. "I shouldn't. I've got inventory figures to go over."

His thumb cruised the back of her hand, and then he brought it to his lips. He turned it and kissed the center, pressing her palm against his cheek, the textures there enticing her. "What are you frightened of, Leigh? Me? Or you?"

His question pursued her as she hurried away, down the halls and up the elevator to her suite, all the time trapping that warm intimate kiss in her fist.

Later, unable to work, Leigh stood by the windows over-looking the ocean. A man stood, legs braced against the wind and she knew he was Jarek, fighting his terrible past.

Why did she ache to go to him? To hold him?

Why wouldn't Annabelle leave him alone?

Why did she care so much?

Six

It had been a long two weeks since Jarek had talked with Leigh and mid-June's tourists had already filled the Amoteh resort's sculpted parking lot and garage.

After finishing the shop, he'd only glimpsed Leigh, who was busy with customers, displays and stocking inventory—all at the same time. When he came to take care of the Stepanov displays, she had made a point of avoiding him. To say that he wasn't feeling bruised would be untrue. To say that he didn't hunger for her would be a lie, but he held his pride dear.

Jarek knew by the sudden stiffening of Leigh's body that she knew he was near. She was in his blood, and unless he had badly mistaken her reaction to him, he was in hers.

But Leigh's decisions were her own.

At dusk, with the sun settling into the Pacific's horizon, Jarek revved the motorcycle up the slight hill and then eased down into the resort's parking lot. After her reaction to his delivery of her parents, Leigh probably wouldn't be happy to discover that the passenger behind him was her brother. And "Winter Child" wasn't in a good mood.

With a California tan, the spoiled and selfish surfer depended on Leigh to send him money and keep him out of scrapes. On a side trip, prior to collecting Ed and Bliss, Jarek had made it a point to discuss family responsibility issues with Ryan. Ryan had agreed, under pressure, to come to Amoteh, but he'd asked for time to say goodbye to his friends. Jarek had slapped a mild threat and an airline ticket into his hand and Ryan had looked at it as if it were dung.

But he'd arrived at Seattle's Sea-Tac airport as he'd promised. His grumbling from behind Jarek had continued on the drive to Washington's southern shores.

When Jarek parked, Ryan swung off the back seat, unfastened his helmet and geared up to dislike Amoteh. "There's no surf here. Not like Down Under or in Hawaii," Ryan stated flatly, his handsome well-tanned face in a frown.

He fluffed his sun-lightened curls, spirals longer than Leigh's, and took in the jutting, modern resort overlooking the rolling ocean. Ryan skimmed the small town of Amoteh, the tourist pier and the boats moored at the other piers. He appraised the sight in two flat words, "Podunk, U.S.A."

"Get to like it. You're here for the summer." Jarek fastened both helmets to his Harley and braced himself for the woman walking quickly across the parking lot. Beneath the big fringed scarf tied around her hips, her dark gray short skirt had hitched up slightly.

He admired those long legs for just a minute before she stood in front of him. She panted slightly, her hands pushed back her jacket and braced on her waist. The pristine white blouse held softness that Jarek ached to caress.

He studied the Hawaiian print of the scarf knotted around her hips. The fringes of the triangular folded garment caught the wind and brushed sensually against those long legs. Leigh followed his admiring study and frowned. "It's a 'pareu.' Some people call it a 'sarong.' It can be tied around the chest or the hips. It matches a bikini…used for a poolside cover-up…one size fits all…hand-washable blend, colorfast.''

Jarek had an image of her wearing the transparent, brightly colored pareu and nothing else. He was glad for the cool mist that had begun to roll into land, foretelling rain; images of Leigh's sultry, sensual looks sent his blood simmering. ''Looks nice with the suit.''

But Leigh had focused on her younger brother. ''Ryan, this is out of your surfing range, isn't it? I thought I sent you enough money to keep out of trouble, and not bother Ed and Bliss.''

''Hey. I didn't come willingly. Big bro here laid a guilt trip on me.''

Leigh pivoted to Jarek, slowly taking in his black leather jacket, worn jeans and boots. ''Now what have you done, Jarek?''

''Explained a few facts of life.''

Ryan added to Jarek's brief statement. ''He thinks you're working too hard and that I need to do my share and keep up the family gig with Ed and Bliss.''

Leigh's fine dark eyebrows lifted. ''Oh, he did, did he?''

Jarek nodded toward Ed and Bliss's small house on the distant hill and shoved Ryan's small duffel bag into his stomach. ''Your parents' place is over there. You're staying there and pitching in with what needs to be done. Remember, you're not to ask them—or Leigh—for any money, and you gave your word to stay put. The front porch needs fixing and they need help with the gardening. Make sure you pick up after yourself.''

Ryan hunched beneath his light jacket and looked at the pavement.

Leigh frowned at her brother. ''I know that look. You're thirty-one now, and it hasn't changed since you were three. You're guilty of something. What is it? What's he got on you, Ryan? How much?''

Ryan scanned the brooding clouds rolling into shore, foretelling rain. "I heard it rains here all the time. He paid peanuts, if you're so interested, and I'm doomed to nowhere for the summer. Some of us were having a party. We trashed a hotel room, okay? No big deal. Dude paid the tab and now I've got to work it off in some crummy furniture factory, six days a week. In all my spare time, when I'm dragging my bones, I get to help Ed and Bliss plant a garden and take care of a house, do their little errands for them, fetch and carry. How much are they paying slaves these days, anyway?"

"You keep what you earn. Lose that job and we'll see how you do at cutting bait. After that, it's scraping barnacles off boat hulls, so the furniture job is cushy in comparison…. You can have this happy family reunion without me. Seven o'clock in the morning, Ryan. Be at the furniture shop." Jarek swung up on his motorcycle and revved it into life. Prowling out of the parking lot, he caught a glance of Leigh, waving her hands and pacing back and forth, apparently lecturing Ryan.

Ryan's bored look said he wasn't listening; Jarek intended that he would in the next few months. Leigh had carried the entire family for long enough. The sight of her now, those dark circles under her eyes, that pale taut look wasn't only from anger—she'd been working too hard to support her family.

Or, he brooded, she was staying up late to take Morris's calls. According to Mikhail, Leigh's boss regularly sent flowers and her suite telephone was usually busy. With overnight mail deliveries, Leigh was apparently keeping up her regular duties as well.

Instead of going to his home, Jarek drove his motorcycle to the workshop. After dealing with Ryan's childish attitude and seeing Leigh, drained from work—and that pareu-thing around her curved hips—he needed the reassuring slide of good solid wood beneath his hands and the scent of oils and sawdust.

As it always did, the wooden cradle he had completed for Annabelle's surprise birthday present loomed behind the closed storage door. In a forgotten corner and covered by a dusty tarp and a box of clean rags, the cradle was put away at the first miscarriage. When Annabelle had died, Jarek had placed a few keepsakes and photos inside the cradle—he'd kept nothing of the house they'd dreamed of and had shared.

Beside the bedroom set that was due to be picked up soon, the unfinished table was his design. A little lighter style than Fadey's chunkier one, it bore the Stepanov look of sturdy, plain furniture meant to last for generations. Extended, it ran to twelve feet, with built-in drawers for silverware and place mats. In the Stepanov tradition, wooden dowels, not metal screws would make it stand and last. Jarek liked to think of that family, growing up and sharing life around his table. The Danish oil finish he'd chosen would cure and harden, and would be best for repairing of inevitable scratches and wear. The bright workshop lights hit the table's fine wood and threw Jarek's reflection back up at him.

He ran the cleaning rag across it. With stubble darkening his jaw and his eyes in shadows, his reflection looked as if he were haunted—maybe he was, with the past and with the unsteady future. If he loved again as deeply as he suspected, he just might find pain, because Leigh had made it clear that she had little room in her life for him.

Well, after she came to tell him to mind his own business, *then* she would have nothing to do with him.

The problem was—the soft feeling and the excitement running inside him told him that she was his business. He wanted to take care of her and that instinct ran too deep to ignore.

Working with the table, seeing it come to life piece by piece, didn't distract him from thinking about Leigh. After closing up the shop hours later, he walked to the Seagull's Perch. There, amid friends and the glass balls and fishing net decorations, he found Lars Anders nursing a mug of beer as he brooded at the end of the bar. As Henry, the bartender, slid a bottle of beer down the long polished length of bar, Jarek caught Lars's glare of pure hatred. Ignoring Lars as he always did, Jarek lifted the bottle; he smoothed away the damp mark on the bar with his hand, appreciating his father's fine restorative work. The bar had come from rip-roaring San Francisco days; it spoke of the Barbary Coast, of sailors crashing into port, and Fadey had loved it back into an elegant gleaming length.

Jarek caught the flash of metal and glanced down the bar to find Lars' knife at work, etching the smooth finish. Lars knew exactly how to pick a fight, and Jarek was just in the mood to oblige—but he wouldn't, because he needed to save himself for Leigh's sure-to-come visit. Ryan had wanted to be dropped off at Ed and Bliss's immediately, but in this case, Jarek thought it best to let "Precious" see her brother first.

Women, he thought darkly, and settled into a good, healthy brood about the intricacies and difficulties of dealing with the opposite sex—one in particular.

Then Lars's voice carried across the bar. "That woman up at your brother's fancy resort. You think she's sleeping with him? Or maybe she's sleeping with her boss, too? The florist told someone that her boss sends flowers all the time. Or maybe a pretty woman like that needs taming from a real man—me."

Rita, with a tray of empty glasses in her hand, came close to whisper to Jarek, "He's in a bad mood. Just paid a heavy fine for running without lights at night and Norma Lou isn't putting up with him anymore—she moved his stuff out of her apartment, and he's out to make someone pay. Don't let him get to you."

Jarek watched Lars slam the point of his knife into the fine wood once more.

"You're too late. He's already way past my tolerance level," he told Rita as he wrapped a bar towel around one fist—small protection from the knife—and moved toward Lars.

As he ducked the beefier man's first punch, Jarek's thoughts were almost detached and very logical. A brawl with Lars was almost the perfect end to a tension-filled day where no one was happy.

Lars didn't fight well and in the end, prompted by Jarek, he'd apologized to Henry and paid for the damage to the bar.

At eleven o'clock, Jarek lay on his bed, showered and wearing his jeans, his arms behind his head. The satisfaction of taking Lars down wasn't there, only the empty night, the rain snaking down the windows and the wind's music in the chimes Bliss had given him. Crafted by her, the spoons hung by the handles and jingled merrily.

He smiled grimly as a bell tinkled lightly near his front door. Whoever had just come up his steps had broken the small thread purposely strung between the two railings. It was a small prevention against a man who wanted revenge; however, Lars and his crew wouldn't have knocked or come straight up to the front door.

Jarek surged off the bed. On a night like this, people usually called first. Whoever it was—

He tugged open the door and a heavy gust drove Leigh against him. In a dressy, full-length city raincoat buttoned to her throat, she held an inside-out umbrella. Her hair had flattened into waving strands around her cheeks.

Jarek held her with one arm, and closed the door behind her with his other hand. Everything he wanted rested close against him. "I missed you," he said truthfully, as stunned, she looked up at him and the umbrella slipped to the floor.

"I…I missed you, too," she whispered unevenly, washing away all the times he'd seen her and she'd turned from him. Her free hand moved to skim his cheekbone, bruised by Lars's fist. "You've been hurt. I'd heard that you were—defending me. Are you hurt badly?"

"I hurt when I'm not with you," he stated plainly, tossing away all caution on a night that the wind and the rain had delivered him the woman he desired. She'd caught the fresh scent of the night's wild storm, tangled it with her own feminine one, and served him a spell he couldn't ignore.

He couldn't move as she traced his eyebrows, eased his damp hair back from his face. On tiptoe, she leaned against him and smoothed the swelling bruise lightly with her lips. "I wish you wouldn't fight. Promise me you won't again, please?"

"Is that why you came? To make me promise?" His lips tasted the rain and the hunger on hers.

"Promise," she whispered desperately. "Promise me now."

"I can't. Not with Lars. He isn't someone you can avoid, not when he's been drinking."

"You were there, too—drinking."

"I was alone and the night was long. I went to see friends, not to drink."

She frowned slightly and pushed away from him, turning to cross her arms in front of her, facing out to the ocean and the night. He came to stand behind her, just to be close to her once more. "What else do you want?"

A flash of lightning tore through the storm, and she turned to him, her face in shadows. "I can't make any promises for Ryan. He's…uh…unreliable. I want to pay you back for whatever money you've paid. I'm low on funds right now, but I—"

"Stop it." He eased his fingers through her wet hair and thought how wonderful she was, fighting for her family, and how much he ached for her. "You'll have to let him grow up sometime, love. He's made a promise, and he'll stick to it. That money will be deducted from his check."

"You don't know him. He uses Ed and Bliss to get to me, and I can't withstand that."

"Ryan understands that he has to carry his own weight here. He has to grow up. He can't do that with you running protection for him. Either he will, or he won't. Either *you'll let him,* or you won't. What concerns me is that you and I have settling to do. This is between just you and me."

"Yes, I know." Once more, Leigh turned to the storm and

the night, away from him, and he waited for her to choose.
Either she'd leave, or she'd—

"I'm so terrified of you. Of what you could mean," she
whispered, turning to look up at him. "I can't just do as I
want. I have responsibilities."

"Tell me how you felt just now, when the wind threw you
against me, when I looked into your eyes and found what I've
been hunting."

"I came to—" She looked away into the lightning's flash
and began again. "I came to make you see that you can't
interfere with my life. Mikhail said you were hurt because of
me. I've been taking care of myself a long time, Jarek. Gossip
means nothing to me, not when it isn't true. I know what that
bully said."

Again, she turned to him and delivered her flat statement.
"I don't sleep with Morris. I wouldn't trade my body for a
position, no matter how badly I wanted it. He's not that kind
of man anyway. But I have had an affair, if you can call weeks
of experimental flirtation and dating and fifteen minutes of sex
in the copy room, an affair."

Leigh hesitated, then shook her head. In the shadows her
expression was sad as if she'd worried in the past and could
find no satisfaction in what had happened. "I knew better than
to date someone in the same office, but Kevin pursued me—
I suppose I was thrilled at the time, to be recognized as a
woman. That fifteen minutes of sex was consensual, disillu-
sioning and painful. And my fault. I had an hour lunch break,
so did he. He asked. I wanted the experience and him, I suppose, looking back…rather like an acquisition to prove I was
a woman. Then Kevin bragged about it, and tried to blackmail
me into bonuses, positions, whatever. I told Morris everything
and Kevin was fired instantly. I work hard. I always have."

Jarek didn't want to think about Kevin and that copy room.
Leigh should have had more. "I know, you work too hard.
But now, maybe it's time for yourself. You'll have to decide."

"You like to play. I don't."

Jarek smoothed those silky curls, enjoying the softness that was Leigh. "Maybe you don't know how."

"No, I suppose not. I don't know that I have time to learn, or want to. You believe me, don't you?"

He would always believe her. Leigh wasn't a woman to deceive. Was he deceiving himself? "Maybe you're not the only one afraid of what moves between us."

"Annabelle," she stated quietly, understanding immediately. "You're still grieving for her, Jarek. You're still wrapped in guilt. I…don't think I can act as a stand-in for your wife. Don't ask me to."

"She has nothing to do with this." Bending to her lips, Jarek whispered, "Only you and I."

She'd been so angry at Jarek for delivering Ryan to Amoteh. She'd always tried to keep business and family apart, and now her entire family was nearby. Trouble that could disrupt the tentative good start she'd made in the shop could erupt at any moment—especially with Ryan's now-surly temper. Mikhail might not be as understanding as Morris; she could lose that bonus and perhaps Morris's faith in her.

Earlier that day, Ryan's lashing bitterness had caused her own temper. "You're siding with that tough dude, aren't you?" he'd demanded.

"You just don't worry Ed and Bliss. Ed still hasn't recovered his strength yet. Bliss is definitely menopausal. She won't admit to hot flashes or her moods and she feels guilty about sometimes snarling at Ed. But they seem to have been accepted by the town. They're comfortable in that house and Bliss says it has good vibes. I've got more than I can do now without chasing after them, but that is secondary to their well being. *Do not upset them, Ryan.*"

"Or? Or what will you do about it? You're always lecturing me. I'm sick of it, and I don't want to know about Bliss's menopause," he had sneered at her. "When has this family ever put down roots? When were we like other kids? Didn't you notice our parents have a little different lifestyle? Like, man. How did you expect me to turn out—like you? All nervous and tired and working day and night? Telling everyone else how to live their lives? Not me, sis. I'm going with the flow, just like Ed and Bliss. If I hadn't promised Big Mean Dude, I wouldn't be here now. He said it was up to me, and maybe I didn't used to have it in me to keep promises—I do now. I'm all grown up now, Precious Blossom. I don't lie and I don't break promises.''

The battle of older sister against a rebelling younger brother had continued on the path to Ed and Bliss's. Bliss's tie-dye T-shirts had been hung over the picket fence, a small young goat fiercely tugging at one. Ed's stone polisher had stood on top of a wood table, his work tools scattered on the ground. Ryan and Leigh's power struggle had stopped at the sight of their parents, holding hands as they stood in the evening breeze, looking worn and faded and glowing with happiness.

''Don't you dare hurt them, Ryan,'' Leigh had whispered fiercely between her teeth as she forced a smile at their parents.

His snarled ''Lay off'' had not been comforting.

She'd just gotten back to her suite at Amoteh Resort and had returned Morris's call, when Mikhail had appeared at her door. She'd thrown a toweling robe over the bikini she was trying on, to see if the special lining in the white triangular cups concealed as it should, for women with dark nipples. For testing purposes, she had covered her own with circles cut from a brown paper sack.

Dressed immaculately in a suit, Mikhail had seemed disturbed. ''I don't suppose you have heard from Jarek, have you? He's been hurt and since the topic of contention was you, I thought you might have an insight—''

''What?'' A kaleidoscope of nightmares had hit her—Jarek, bandaged in the emergency ward, Jarek, lying in a pool of blood—and fear for him had chilled her.

In his efficient, click-click business manner, Mikhail had relayed the details of Jarek upholding her honor at the local bar. She had wondered why he grinned as she tore off the robe and replaced it with her raincoat. He had not moved from her pathway soon enough, and Leigh was astounded that she had pressed the tip of the umbrella into his midsection and ordered, "Move it, buddy."

Courteous as always, Mikhail's expression had been amused. He had bowed slightly, formally. "Certainly."

As she had hurried down the hall, she thought she heard his chuckle. But she had had no time for Mikhail, not when Jarek had been hurt. She'd had to find him and—

She'd definitely found Jarek. From desperate worry to mind-stunning happiness, she'd found him. A gust of wind had thrown her into his arms and she forgot all her reservations, all her problems—Ryan, Ed's recovery and Bliss's mood swings. Looking up at him, held tightly against him, she had forgotten about how much the Amoteh contract with Bella Sportswear would mean.

In the shadows of his spartan home, Jarek was warm and alive and safe. In that moment, when the wind had thrown her against him and the wind chimes' musical sound had mixed with that of the storm, Leigh had felt complete, as if she'd found peace at last.

Leigh closed her eyes as Jarek's lips cruised hers, warming away the storm's chill. Or was it the past sliding away and a new beginning waiting for her, with the rain pounding Jarek's small home, the wind howling around it. In the sound of the wind chimes and in the pounding of her heart, she knew she would make love with Jarek that night.

She arched up against him, locking her fists in that waving hair, holding him as she dived into sensations, textures and pleasure—rough skin against her own, big, broad, wonderfully strong and gentle hands framing her face. Was the fierce tempo of the storm outside, or was it within her body and her heart?

He gathered her closer and one hand slid inside her raincoat to—

Jarek pulled away slightly and grinned. "A bikini."

His tone was a combination of sensuality, hunger and a little boy's delight with a present on Christmas morning. While Jarek's gaze warmed and circled and tightened the tiny muscles low in her body, she heard herself speak, automatically reciting Bella's catalog description— "White, with the very best of linings, a double weave in nude tone to hide shadows. I was just testing it when Mikhail—"

She held her breath as he slowly unbuttoned her coat, easing it open. His grin slid into desire as he slowly removed and tossed it aside.

Jarek's big, work-hardened hands skimmed her shoulders, her arms and lower. That dark intent gaze grazed hers, and his hands slid to her back, tugging free the bow tied there, and then so slowly up to her nape.

The brown paper sack circles fluttered to the floor unnoticed as Leigh's heart hammered and stilled and opened. Beneath her hands, his bare chest was smooth and warm, his heart racing in rhythm to hers. She'd never seen a man so affected, so intent as Jarek touched her gently, reverently—a slight pressure at her waist that skimmed to her hips, the opening of those big soft hands to hold her. One by one, he tugged the bows free at her hips. The silky cloth slid down her thighs, pale and soft and fragile, just as she felt.

In the shadows, Jarek studied the tangle of cloth, then the arrogance and the pride was back as his gaze ripped up to hers. He didn't move or speak, and she knew that he wasn't going to touch her again—unless she wanted him, too.

"Yes," she whispered, fearing even as she desired. "Yes," she repeated unevenly, her body heating as she moved against him and kicked off her shoes.

She heard the sound of his breath and knew that he had been holding it, then his lips were on hers, demanding, fiery, as stormy and fierce as the night outside.

Leigh met him, used her strength to hold him, caught the tempo of hunger inside him and returned it with her own. She heard a long, uneven sigh of pleasure, and recognized it as her own. It had come from an emotion so deep and true that she hadn't known it existed. She heard her blood rush through her body, and threw herself into the heat that was Jarek.

She sensed his fierce need, felt his arms carry her to his bed, clung to him when he would have moved away. When he would have come gently to her, she arched against him. Each touch, each heartbeat heightened her need, no gentle, controlled emotion. Whatever she'd been seeking was hers, now...here with Jarek, the intensity, the passion, the truth.

The rhythm ran on, racing without her control as Jarek shuddered and caressed and pressed her beneath him, his hands smoothing her breasts, cherishing them until she ached. He whispered unevenly against her skin, his shoulders broad and strong enough to carry her where they both would go.

Then, braced above her, shoulders outlined by a lightning flash, his face was honed, harsh, so real, passion written clearly on each plane and shadow. The primitive truth said she was his, and he was hers, and she would have no less.

Whatever she had been, she forgot, the constraints, the shoulds and should nots. Now there was only Jarek, hard and full against her, the heat rising between them as he bent to take her breast gently—

She cried out, in desperation and in passion and Jarek was there, safe in the storm, holding her tight, his body flowing with hers perfectly. She couldn't stop, restrain the tempo, the rising struggle to reach outside and beyond herself. Again Jarek whispered against her cheek, his deep voice passionate and uneven as his lips burned hers and she fought the pleasure, then welcomed it with a high, wild cry—*Jarek...Jarek....*

Leigh surfaced slowly, lying blissfully spent against him, her legs tangled with his and held him tight, an anchor in an unsafe new world. With her head resting on his shoulder, his arm around her and his fingers smoothing her hair, she tried to find answers and couldn't. She only heard the slow, certain beat of his heart and the rain pattering against the windows. It was a good time, she thought drowsily, a good feeling to be held by Jarek. She gathered him closer, keeping him from his haunting heartache and the woman who called to him from long ago.

This is between you and me.... he'd said.

"Deep thoughts?" Jarek asked softly as he nuzzled her cheek.

"Mmm. You said you sleep sometimes in the display bed. That's because you need somewhere that doesn't remind you of her, isn't it?"

"I custom-made this bed after Annabelle, but the buyers had changed their mind to another style. But sometimes, yes— I badly need sleep—to get away from what was and is—those dreams we had. I relax a bit in a room full of Stepanov furniture. But I always change the sheets later," he added with just that lilt of humor to his voice. His hand drew back her curls and he studied her within his arms. "They named you right, Precious Blossom."

"Sure. If I'm not mistaken, I nipped you once or twice, and I didn't feel very sweet."

"Mmm. It doesn't hurt a man's pride to know that his woman is hungry for him." The statement, wrapped in that slight accent, seemed so like Fadey that Leigh smiled. She yawned and stretched and smiled as Jarek's hand came cruising up to enclose her breast.

"This time, we'll take our time, love. Indulge me. I want to make a good impression," Jarek murmured as he began to caress her once more.

Just before dawn, Leigh rose to draw on her raincoat. She came to the bed to study the man who was now her lover. His eyes opened slowly, as though even in his sleep the sensuality between them snared him. That lazy look held hers and the beautiful kaleidoscope of the night's lovemaking magically bound them.

She took in that tall body, now relaxed and tanned against the plain cotton sheets, that face, rugged and shadowed by the night's beard.

This was her lover, a man who had been intimate with her, whose hands had caressed her restless body and had opened her gently to his need.

Her lover. His lovemaking lingered pleasurably in the humming muscles of her body—as if with one touch the heat and the storm would swirl around them again, recharged once more—and in the peace she couldn't describe.

Jarek's hand reached slowly out to slide up her thigh, caressing her and his dark sensual look said he wanted yet again. He smiled softly and Leigh found herself smiling too. When he rose to his feet, drawing on his jeans, her heart stilled and leaped and raced. She admired his body, the flowing powerful muscles that had held her so gently throughout the night.

Before parting, they stood on his porch, Jarek's arms around her from behind, his hands holding hers.

For the first time in her life, Leigh felt she could stay just like that—with Jarek holding her, her problems in another world. Whatever turmoil she would face, she would know that in that moment, she had found true peace.

His kiss wasn't that of passion, but of something deeper that she both wanted and feared....

As Jarek watched Leigh hurry away, he gripped the rails of his porch hard enough to pale his knuckles. She hadn't wanted him to return with her to the Amoteh Resort, and that meant she was uncertain of appearances—and perhaps her emotions. He sensed her uneasiness as he could sense a storm brewing on a quiet, perfect day.

She disappeared into the fog and he was once more alone. He closed his eyes and saw how she'd looked, making love with him—how softly her body had flowed with his, how strong and desperate she had been, all woman—fiercely intense, matching him in his desire.

Jarek rubbed the ache in his chest, the need to hold her again, and scanned the scene in front of him. The air smelled of rain now, the grass still bent with the wind. The squall had swept over the piers and already people were repairing the

damage done to their boats, or at their shops, working with
torn canvas and signs. An unfamiliar upscale tourist boat was
prowling slowly over the dark swells, and just beyond it, in
the gray dawn and wrapped in fog was Deadman's Rock.

He forced himself to breathe. Chief Kamakani's curse just
could hold true and somehow Leigh could be in danger. But
how?

In the fog concealing Strawberry Island, Kamakani seemed
to be waiting, aching for his homeland and raging against the
slavers who had taken him. Legend said that only a woman
who knew herself well, who could dance the dance of his
forefathers would end the curse.

Jarek forced himself away from that darkness and longed to
hold Leigh once more, to protect her. Yet the sense that everything he'd wanted, held in the night and loved, could be
taken away easily, remained.

Was he haunted? Maybe. But now it was by the sound of
Leigh's pleasure, the silky feel of her skin, her body, the sweet
promise of loving her again and again.

Seven

Leigh smoothed the maillot-style bathing suit and adjusted the splashy pink and red pareu knotted at her hip. It neatly concealed the suit's high-leg cut which disturbed her preference toward dressing in business clothes. Yet wearing Bella Swimwear said that she personally endorsed the designs. This pareu would do, until the Amoteh's special strawberry design arrived.

On the afternoon after making love with Jarek, the fringes brushed sensuously against her leg, reminding her of how he had caressed her—before passion took him. Then he had been fierce, possessive, desperate—but no more than she.

She shivered slightly, still shocked at her own feverish passion. Leigh straightened the designer sunglasses perched on top of her head when they threatened to slide. She found her fist locked to one of the suits on the ladies' size-ten rack. Flattened with the black maillot, her breasts still tingled and hardened from Jarek's mouth.

And she could still feel him deep in the tenderness of her

lower body. Leigh realized she had just sighed hungrily when a lady who had insisted that she was a twelve—and who was more of a sixteen—came from the dressing room, wearing a bikini. Leigh managed a bright smile, selected a larger size in a different pattern and made her way to the woman, who was frowning at her mirrored image. "This design is sized as a sixteen, but it runs really small. I think the color would look fabulous on you. Sea-green will bring out the color of your eyes."

Sea-green. The color of Jarek's eyes, filled with passion and storms and—

"Really?" Pleased with the suit and its apparent wrong sizing, the woman hurried into the dressing room.

Leigh smiled to herself. That customer had already purchased trunks for her husband and grown sons and bathing suits for her grandchildren. On a family vacation, she'd also purchased a hefty gift certificate for her daughters-in-law.

The shop's location, near the massive pool and atrium, was perfect. The store had been open for one week. The young mother who helped part-time was wonderful. Sales were good; not even Mikhail could find fault. He had been adamant that the shop was not open city-hours, but that ten o'clock in the morning until four in the afternoon were enough. "If they want to swim and do not have the sense to pack their suits, that is their problem, not the Amoteh's. We serve beautiful poolside dinners, and I do not want any focus outside of that, no jumping up and running to try on swimsuits. Ten to twelve...one to four, Sundays and Mondays closed. I will not have this resort turned into a shopping mall."

Forcing herself from a night of Jarek's intensity into the business that waited at her suite hadn't been easy. The bath intended to give her a buffer between the two had been interrupted by Morris's call. She'd been blowing the mounds of bubbles away from her well-sated body and just at the point of falling asleep. It had been sinful of course, not to take a quick shower and hurry into her workload of calls and faxes.

When she'd answered the telephone next to the massive tub, she couldn't prevent the happy sigh, or the yawn.

Morris's voice had sounded immediately concerned. "Leigh, you're usually up and sounding crisp by seven o'clock. Is there a problem? Are you ill?"

"I'm fine. More than fine," she had added with a cat-in-cream smile that she felt all through her body and soul.

"Your voice is different…more husky. Have you gotten a cold from all that rain in the area? Maybe you're still sleepy, but you usually sound wide-awake at this hour. Did you work late?"

"Work? No." Leigh lay back in the tub and eased her big toe into the elegant tub spout.

That was a mistake. She'd tried to remove it and carry on business as usual with Morris, who was clearly worried about her. "Stepanov still won't budge, huh? Won't let someone else take over the project?"

"He isn't a man who changes his mind. I'm working with it, Morris. The shop is doing fabulously, but Mikhail isn't the kind of man you push past a certain point."

"I have confidence in you. Leigh? I hear water and you seem out of breath."

"Washing up, just after exercising. I want to look good when wearing Bella fashions. Have to go."

Her toe had still been stuck, and she had furiously massaged the bar of soap around it when Ryan called at seven-thirty. "I hate this place," he had said flatly. "It stinks and there's a whole load of lumber and scrap they want me to unload, and cleaning shelves and taking inventory—by noon, Leigh. The Stepanovs are slave drivers, and Big Dude told me not to bother you. Hey, don't hang up—"

Leigh had not had time to worry about Ryan's disconnected call. She had had her own problems—her toe wasn't budging. She reached for the elegant Amoteh shaped strawberry body oil and began rubbing that on her toe. It wasn't like her to play and relax so completely in a bath—she was a shower-person.

She had settled in to battle her imprisoned toe and to debate how Jarek could easily make her lose focus. She was too susceptible to him. People incorporated lovemaking into their everyday lives and went to work in the morning.

Yet she felt as if her life had flipped over in one month, and now every day was a surprise.

She'd never liked surprises; she liked predictable schedules.

At seven-forty, Bliss had called. From the sound of her voice, she'd been crying. "I didn't know it would be so hot here. These sudden ocean winds must come from the desert somewhere. They make me cranky."

She had sniffed lightly, then exclaimed happily, "Oh, I'm so happy here. We're working in the garden tonight—Winter Child, Ed and me. Come if you can, Precious."

When her toe finally came free, Leigh had hurried to dress and open the shop. The steady flow of customers hadn't given her time to think until she closed at noon. She had had personal business to do—protecting Jarek from Lars. She had to make certain that Lars wouldn't hurt Jarek.

A brisk walk down the Amoteh's steps had taken her to a sleazy small motor repair shop and the apartment above it. Georgia had said that Lars Anders lived there, when in port. Lars had leered at her, but he'd promised not to torment Jarek again, *after* she'd written a hefty check.

Feeling as if she had more of her life in control, and that Jarek was now safe from harm, Leigh had reopened the Bella shop at one promptly.

Now, at the shop's four o'clock closing time, her life was in sync and scheduled again, all the rough edges ironed out. She moved to arrange the hot pink plastic sandals where they would catch the light better, and smiled at the sound of children playing Marco Polo in the pool. The newlywed groom waiting for his bride to emerge from the dressing room was clearly impatient, and the man with a belly overhang really shouldn't have selected those skimpy black trunks.

But the tall man in the black T-shirt and jeans standing next to him would have looked divine without clothing. In contrast to the colorful displays and signs, he looked starkly masculine. With his arms crossed as he leaned against the shop's door, Jarek took in her black suit and pareu, and his dark sultry look said he could devour her just as passionately as last night.

Leigh felt her heart lurch so violently that she covered it with her hand and tried to catch her breath.

The woman trying on sunglasses beside her must have sensed Leigh's sensual tug because she lowered the glasses to peer over the frames.

"Don't even think about it, honey. He's wearing my tag," she whispered in an aside to Leigh. Then she glided toward him as she exclaimed in a sexy, delighted tone, "Darling! I was wondering when I'd see you. You know I just come here when I can to see you."

"Marcella," Jarek returned quietly as his gaze remained locked with Leigh's.

A teenage girl whispered to her mother, "Mom, that's him. That's the hunk I was telling you about. Isn't he gorgeous?"

Her mother smiled. "He's a little too old for you. If I didn't love Daddy so much, I might—"

"Mom!" the shocked teenager exclaimed. "You're just too old to even think about men *like that*. And not Daddy. No. No way do I want to think about that."

The mother's secret smile said that she had plans for the skimpy swimsuit cover-up she'd just purchased; they included a very private session with her husband.

While the man with the belly overhang flexed his muscles in front of the mirror and tried to suck in the flab, Marcella had latched her arms around Jarek's shoulders and lifted her face for a kiss.

Leigh's sandals locked to the floor, her hands to the counter, as her entire body riveted to the sight of Marcella's lithe, and obviously enhanced body against Jarek's muscular one. Without making a sound, Leigh felt the primitive hissing inside her, much like a cat would make while arching its back, hair bristling in a threat—yet she hadn't moved.

Jarek removed Marcella's twining arms without looking away from Leigh. He shook his head when Marcella whispered something throaty and inviting, and held up her room card-lock. The reminder that Jarek appealed to women nettled Leigh. Why should he be interested in her—make love with her—when women were waiting to give him their room cards?

Leigh couldn't explain her own fierce, possessive anger, and she didn't like that dark emotion. She'd seen other women display it and at the time, had thought it was silly and showy.

She automatically explained the fine quality used in the men's trunks to a woman customer even as her anger and suspicions grew. She was probably just another woman, another conquest on Jarek's list, despite what he'd said about loving his wife and abstaining from sex.

He certainly hadn't abstained last night. Leigh punched the cash register purchases, made an error that took time to correct and tried to dampen her rising temper. Jarek could bring out all sorts of unexpected and dark emotions, and that nettled her. She seemed to be skipping from one emotion to another. She'd become an elemental woman, and her control was slipping, and it was Jarek's fault.

When the last customer left, Jarek locked the door and walked toward her.

"Did you *ever* go to bed with that woman?" Leigh's jealous tone surprised her, so did her anger. She hurried to rummage in her bag for her checkbook, and quickly scrawled a check made out to him. "There. I don't want anyone to think that last night was some sort of payment for my parents' rent. That amount should be sufficient."

"I don't lie. I said what happened was between you and me, and I meant it. I never touched her, or any other woman since my wife, until last night." His deep voice was curt, pride

and arrogance slashing at her. He took the check, tore it up
and slammed the pieces on the glass counter with enough force
to shake the sunglasses display.

She caught the rack and straightened it. She'd been so
wrapped in her own emotions that she hadn't noticed Jarek's
own dark mood. But now, all the bristling edges were there,
the taut muscle moving in his jaw, that grim, beautiful mouth,
the danger that seemed to crackle around his taut body.

The impact of that anger took Leigh back one step, her
senses taut. "Is there a problem?"

He reached to remove the designer sunglasses perched on
top of her head and tossed them to a jumble of turquoise-
colored suits. "Just you."

Even now, with his dark mood storming him, Jarek wanted
her. Maybe it was his Russian blood that brooded and simmered and nagged at his pride. Maybe it was because she'd
hurt him. How silly that sounded, a little slip of a woman with
frothy, silky hair and big honey-colored eyes and just the light-
est touch of freckles running across her nose, could hurt him—
could tear right into the heart of him and wound him and
everything he was, or tried to be.

How could he say that in words—that she'd hurt him? Instead anger was better—and rules as to how to treat a lover,
and a man.

Maybe it was better. He noted Leigh's slight frown, her
uncertainty and his anger wavered.

"You've had a busy day already, haven't you? To say nothing of last night. You still had enough energy to pay a noon-
time visit to Lars at his apartment. And now everyone in Amoteh knows you bought him off—made a deal with him and
paid him not to 'hurt' me…. *Not to 'hurt' me,*" he repeated.

The dig to his pride went deeper to fester. "I was brought
up to take care of my own battles, my own life. Is that what
you do for Ryan, Leigh? Maybe that's why he's spoiled and
lazy. I'm not. You're not going to adopt me as one of the

people you have to protect and provide and nurture. I've been managing for quite a while."

"I thought I could help. He's a bully—"

"That's right, he is. And the way to handle bullies is to deal with them, not buy them off."

"At least you'll be safe," she stated firmly, her arms crossing protectively in front of her chest.

Jarek rammed his hand through his hair. He hadn't known women could be so unaware of a man's pride. Either he kept it, or he didn't. And if he didn't, he had nothing.

"It's all very silly, you know. He promised, and now he won't taunt you," she said firmly.

Lars had taunted him after Annabelle's death—that he should have taken better care of his wife. That fight was far more savage than the one at the bar and yet Lars couldn't resist taunting him last night. It was in his nature to hurt and Annabelle's death had given him that leverage. More than likely, Leigh wouldn't understand bitterness than ran deep and black and savage. Maybe Jarek could make her understand something else— "Oh, no, he won't say anything…not to my face. He'll just be spreading the word in every port, in every bar that I'm hiding behind a woman's checkbook. Now what implication does that have? That *I'm* getting paid for services?"

"You know that's not true. I just wanted you safe. The same way as I want my parents safe and Ryan, too. I thought money was the way to reach him."

That was something—she'd included him in her realm of people that she loved. "Ryan has to grow up and he can't do it with you fending for him," he said more gently, because he realized that Leigh cared. "Let him make his own life. I'll get your buy-off money back. I won't have that on my conscience."

"I've been taking care of Ryan since forever. I was three when he was born. He hasn't complained about me helping him financially. And I didn't mean to insult you, or infer that you couldn't take care of yourself," she added stiffly. "Don't you dare approach Lars about that money. It was a business deal and it's done."

"Oh, but I will. I just came first to see you, to see if it was true."

"Do, and I'll—"

She was right on the edge, just as she had been last night— just as passionate, just as ready, and just as fascinating. Those gold eyes flashed, her color rising, that soft mouth trembling—

Jarek couldn't resist toying with her curls, letting the silky texture twine around his finger. Now *she* was simmering, clearly in a very enchanting snit. "You take away something very important when you make Ryan dependent on you, Precious. Let him earn his own way. He'll still love you."

Because Ryan hadn't ever met responsibilities, he'd been sulky and snappy and childish—until Fadey picked him up and placed him on a workbench. Fadey had stuck a lollipop in Ryan's hand. "You act like a child—you get treated as a child. Sit there, boy, until you mind better and keep your mouth busy with that candy instead of whining."

"Me? Whine?" Ryan had croaked indignantly, his body stiffened to fight.

Fadey's big palm had landed on top of Ryan's head, waggling it playfully. "Work is good for men. Children play and men work. I treat you like my sons, no less, no more. You work—we'll be fine. You don't work—I treat you like baby. Make up your mind, little boy."

Jarek could have told Ryan what would happen when he tried to leave his perch on the workbench. Fadey's big rough hand had caught the back of his neck and held him there. He had shaken Ryan easily. "Behave, little boy. Maybe I teach you how to make surfboard later when you do the work you must and when you know the tools better."

"Huh? You will?" Ryan's interest had been piqued.

With his back to Ryan, Fadey had grinned at Jarek, shrugged, and whispered, "How difficult can a surfboard be to make? To start, one buys a blank form—has some little bit of wood in the center of foam and resin, no? What I don't know, I will learn. Then I will teach…. Some give, some take, but rules always—right and wrong—that is how you were raised, too. He's just a little late catching up, eh?''

"Okay, Pop. I can handle anything you throw at me,'' Ryan had stated stubbornly.

Fadey had winked at Jarek before turning. "Do not be so certain, boy. No man has ever outworked Fadey Stepanov. You think you can? Show me. You see how my son works hard? Jarek makes good furniture that will stand for families even when he is gone. My son is a man.''

Jarek had smiled at his father's pride and knew he'd inherited it and a certain amount of old-fashioned arrogance. Was it arrogant to want the woman he held in his arms last night, to feel her blood rushing to meet his, to want her to look at him as she did this morning?

Was it arrogant to want more of her, to hold and adore her? To want to inhale her scent as she lay tangled with him in his bed?

He had shrugged mentally, because he knew what he wanted—Leigh, the woman, his woman.

"I take care of my family,'' Leigh was saying, settling in to sulk. With her arms crossed in front of her, the top of her breasts surged over the tight maillot's scoop neckline and the soft flesh quivered as she moved.

He could have picked her up and hurried to the closest dressing room door—one with a good lock on it, his body already hardened, sensitized to the heartbeat along her throat, to the memory of the heat inside her….

"I like bikinis better. But this one-piece thing is nice, too.'' He wanted her with no clothing at all, rich and soft and flowing and hot.

Leigh's sulky pout reminded him of Ryan. Her body reminded him of the woman he'd made love to last night and this morning, who met the day with him, snuggled back in his arms.

"I want to know what you think of me," she whispered, looking away from him. "We've known each other only a short time and—I'm not the kind of woman who sleeps around."

He bent to nuzzle her throat, find that woman scent there. "I think we have waited for each other and now time means nothing. I think you are sweet and loving and I am honored that you would let me love you."

Those fabulous eyes opened wide, and Leigh's body quivered. "You think that?"

Jarek truly loved Leigh's little quivers. They were honest, feminine and fascinating.

"I want you alone—now," he whispered as he bent to brush his lips across hers. He realized the statement was a command, a bit arrogant, a bit too macho even as he said it. But with Leigh, he didn't feel like the contemporary, obliging, equal rights male—he felt like a man with a strong woman who could hold her own with him. Either she would oblige— because she wanted to, or she would refuse.

When she inhaled and stood statue-still, he changed the slant and the tender, seeking mood. In his stark desire for Leigh, he found the hunger he had to have, the woman inside who called to his heart.

He continued kissing her as he back-walked her into a dressing booth and closed the tall shuttered doors behind them. He sat with Leigh on his lap and opened the hunger that had been prowling through him since this morning. Not even his simmering anger about Lars had waylaid that passion, the need to hold her close.

She was hot and taut and hungry against him, her fingers in his hair, her mouth lush and open on his own, her body trembling as he caressed the curves flattened by the suit. He smiled slightly against her breasts as that wonderful, pleasure-hungry sigh purred out of her and her hand tugged up his T-shirt to smooth his chest.

Jarek sighed; it was good to be wanted, to have her hands exploring him—

The sharp rap at the door found Jarek's fingers prowling beneath the high-cut elastic. Leigh stilled against him, her eyes wide and panicked.

Only Mikhail's brother would recognize the humor in his voice. "The waiters are preparing the poolside tables and the evening's entertainment. Unfortunately the guests will have an excellent view of the only way out of this shop. I suggest you exit now."

"I'm just adjusting the mirror," Jarek said and grinned at Leigh who looked as if she couldn't move.

Mikhail whistled on his way out and at the click of the lock, Leigh jumped to her feet and slid into her discarded sandals. Her expression was adorable—her cheeks were flushed, partly from their passion and then from realizing just where she was and what she was doing. She tugged up her swimsuit as Jarek sat, drawing her to stand between his knees, his hands beneath the fringed fabric, smoothing her hips.

"I love how you smell. That woman scent." He trailed kisses over the tops of her breasts and nuzzled the enticing crevice. When he opened his mouth on each nipple, suckling gently, Leigh gasped. But she held him tight, and that mooring gentled the desire within him. "Come with me."

The husky invitation snared at her senses, but she couldn't. "I have work to do. One of the offices just lost a manager and I have to go over résumés...."

Jarek reached to frame that wonderful, expressive face within his hands. He gave her what was in his heart, even though he knew she would refuse. "Then come live with me."

Clearly stunned, she hesitated and then shook her head. "You know that I can't."

"To me, it is simple. Either you want me, or you don't. But

I am not a man for hiding what I feel. I won't sneak behind corners, trying to catch a minute of your time."

"You had more than a few minutes last night," she reminded him very carefully.

He sensed her backing away from him, putting up barriers when he saw none. To Jarek, living together after lovemaking was a natural consequence.

To live life together, forever, was fate.

"Perhaps you need to know exactly how I feel," he said, trying to find the words to make Leigh understand. "And this isn't the place."

"You're moving too fast for me, Jarek. I have—"

He released her face; her decisions were her own. "I know—responsibilities and schedules. Make room in there someplace for me, will you?" he asked sarcastically before rising. He wouldn't beg her for time. "Either you want me, or you don't."

He knew that he was being unreasonable; but then, he allowed himself that—after all, he wanted her very much. To think that she might not want him hurt badly. With Leigh, his confidence needed reassurance at times. Perhaps it was because he was a Stepanov that when he desired, he wanted everything. Yes, so it was. He was unreasonable, and he wanted her, and he wanted her to want him. Did she?

"How can you be so—so demanding? I have a job—"

He had just stepped out of the dressing booth when Leigh's hand lightly touched his shoulder. "I...I will come with you. I have to go up to my suite first—"

Still bruised by her resistance to the beauty between them, Jarek's pride bound him still. Jealousy prickled his nerves and he didn't like it. "To talk with Morris?"

"To change clothes."

"I suppose then, that I should come with you," he murmured, not exactly pleased to be so inflexible and stiff. It seemed that he was not far from his father's old-world possessiveness when it came to the woman he considered his.

Even now, his blood rushed hot through his veins, needing to have her, to know that she cared. Was he so fragile and vulnerable with her that he needed her reassurance?

Did he need her now to reaffirm that last night's magic really happened?

Yes, the answer whispered back to him as he took her hand and hurried along the halls.

At the Seawind Suite, he tugged a breathless Leigh after him. Unable to wait a heartbeat more, he closed the door, and caught her in his arms.

There. There was the fire and the hunger of his woman, the answering of her blood to his, her body already flowing, ready for his. He could have this fever, if not the certainty she would seek him out because she needed him for gentler reasons.

She never felt more alive, meeting his passion, feeding her own, than when Jarek's hands trembled and he slid her suit from her. He'd whipped away his T-shirt and his hot, hungry look had taken in her body, his head tilted at that arrogant, proud angle.

Then he dropped his hands and stood back, making her choose what would happen between them, making her come after him. To take just that one step toward him, and then still, he didn't hold her. Even as his body obviously needed hers, he stood rigid and waiting, those eyes almost emerald beneath his lowered lids.

What was the ritual that came so naturally to her? The placing of her nude body against his, unashamed in her own hunger, her breasts etching his chest seemed in perfect symphony to her emotions. She moved naturally, luxuriously enjoying her feminine role, caressing him with her body, her hands also at her side.

She hadn't known she could seduce, and Jarek was her temptation, her challenge.

The silent battle raged between them, who would give first, who would—

She slid her hands up and down his chest, watching him, watching her touch heat until the breaking point.

Jarek tensed and sucked in breath, holding it as she lowered her mouth to those mysterious male nipples, tugging at them with her lips, her teeth, until his unwilling groan of desire shook the air around them.

What sort of game was this? What was she doing, a woman who had had no time for games?

She smiled against his chest as the answer came back to her—she was a woman who was taking exactly what she wanted and needed.

"Undress me," he ordered in an uneven rasp that was pure male emotion, sizzling, hot, immediate.

Inexperienced, she fumbled the snap, and groaning with frustration, Jarek quickly took up the task, tearing away his jeans, kicking away his loafers. "Do that again," he whispered raggedly. "Move against me."

It was a ritual she understood and yet could not define.

He needed to know she wanted him.

She needed to know that she was her own woman, setting her terms for equal favors.

Then she stepped back, her heart pounding with anticipation. The sun coming through the massive window outlined Jarek's powerful, tense shoulders, his muscled arms and hips and long legs.

She ached for him to fill her with that heavy proud sensuality—and yet, she waited, her body pulsing, hot, hungry.

"You'll live with me," he said, a statement this time, not a question.

"Don't count on it." She wasn't agreeing until she was ready.

"We'll see, love," he murmured quietly, before tugging her to him. As he kissed her, open and wild, she met him once again, feverish in her own desire.

He tossed her to the bed, and not willing to be taken easily,

Leigh pushed back—staying him with her hands on his chest. "You're not going to manage me with sex."

"I can try, can't I?" he asked with a grin that shocked her. Suddenly from a tense challenge, Jarek had moved into tenderness, watching her as he toyed with her curls. "Come live with me. I am a lonely man. You've ruined me," he teased while nuzzling her cheek with his.

"Oh!" Leigh cried out and grabbed him. Later, she would know that she didn't have the strength to move Jarek's weight, and yet, he let her turn him easily so that she rested on top.

"I thought we might go for a walk along the beach—ummm," he murmured appreciatively as she dived in to take his mouth, to move rhythmically against him.

"Stop talking."

"Okay, Precious." He turned her once more and glanced down at their bodies, tangled, male and female. When he looked at her again, she realized she'd been holding her breath, trying to understand that intent stare at their locked bodies, the tension sizzling in him now apart from sensuality—what was it? she wondered uneasily before Jarek began loving her long and slow and very thorough.

An hour later, she walked with him, hand in hand along the beach, the wind tugging at her jacket and chinos. Leigh thought about all the work she needed to do and flung the thought away into the dark swells rolling toward her, the sand sucking at her bare feet.

When Jarek stopped to pick up a shell, showing it to her, the careless marks of a clam digger ruining the shell and leaving it, she wondered how he must have been as a child, playing on the shore.

He turned to catch her soft look, and without speaking, brushed a kiss across her lips and placed his arms around her, drawing her against him.

She wondered what he thought of, holding her close and

rocking her gently, and then over his shoulder she saw Dead-man's Rock. Jarek still carried that guilt, sharing its depth with no one—but she understood that torment and held him tighter.

Let him go, Annabelle. Free him....

Eight

Leigh couldn't concentrate, not after a week of long, steamy nights with Jarek. He wanted everything, and again there was that flickering look down their bodies, that tender look at her beneath him, the nuzzling of her breasts, and the slow possessive sweep of his hand over her belly.

On the third week of June, business was good—at the shop and with the corporation. Leigh pushed the Bella's corporate inventory list aside and considered her parents' new home. Gleaming white in the afternoon sunshine, it was bordered now by vivid flowers. Small in the distance, Mary Jo was standing beside Bliss, considering the backyard garden, the ocean as a backdrop for the two women. Bliss's long, loose shift caught the wind, just brushing Mary Jo's leggy jeans.

Despite different pasts, they seemed so much in tune with each other—women planning a garden, sharing with each other. Ed and Bliss seemed happy enough for now.

Ryan was still sulking. When she saw he and Jarek easing a heavy armoire into the Stepanov showroom, her brother had

glared at her. He'd caught Jarek's look at Leigh and her re-
sulting blush, and Ryan wasn't one to spare feelings when he
was unhappy. It was only a matter of time before they would
argue, and as explosive as Ryan could be, the ricocheting
sparks could hurt Ed and Bliss.

Leigh sighed restlessly, and felt guilty about the work she'd
put aside last night to be with Jarek.

Jarek. Hard, commanding, vibrant, enticing, playful—
tender, romantic, almost savagely possessive.

Come live with me. She hadn't moved in with him, and yet
every night found her in his arms, that delicious hunger taking
them and the world spinning as if nothing else mattered.

Leigh sipped the iced juice drink on her desk. She glanced
at the figures that said Bella shops would succeed in the Amoteh. She managed to cram more paperwork into her slow hours
at the shop, making more time to spend with Jarek.

She studied the figures again, checking them. Even open
just five hours a day, with a healthy tourist markup—Mikhail
did not want "cheap, discount goods" in his resort—the profit
margin was high....

Her thoughts swung back to Jarek and tiny sparks ignited
throughout her body, that tightening of her muscles when she
thought of him, filling her so tightly, becoming one, moving
as one, toward one goal. With Jarek, lovemaking could swing
from tender to primitive, and total possession. Slowly erotic,
one light touch trailing over her skin could make her ache.
His body tensing beneath her skimming hands could set off
an instant reaction.

Who possessed whom? Leigh wondered. She was as possessive, fiery, igniting with him, her skin burning every time
he touched her. Now, her body was so attuned to his that she
could sense him near, almost feel his touch on her skin, electricity seeming to dance between them, even at a distance. The
sensual war between Jarek and herself had caused her appetite
to zip from healthy to ravenous. Every muscle felt toned and

ready for his lovemaking, poised for the next time she would see him.

She frowned slightly, uncomfortable with her new sensations, the hunger prowling through her. *Come live with me....*

Jarek meant more than sleeping with him at night. How could she possibly share a home and therefore, a life with Jarek? There would be obligations on both sides, time, energy and loyalty constraints. Business and family—her family— would make that difficult. And Jarek was not a man to live in the background, he was passionate, vital, arrogant, and stormy arguments were certain to flash between them. She was scheduled; Jarek was impetuous, ready to enjoy life at the moment's opportunity.

He was edgy, brooding, happy, and the tumultuous combination would have her—what? Excited? Fascinated? Grasping for life on the edge, experiencing it to the fullest with Jarek?

Leigh tapped her pen on a stack of unsigned papers which she had to fax back to the main office. She couldn't ignore her workload; Morris depended on her. She scrubbed her hands over her face, feeling the pressure as she always did, yet also feeling a call within her to go to Jarek, to be with him.

Lust? Definitely.

Tenderness? Of course, that, too.

Understanding? No, she didn't understand herself, or what was happening to her...how she could throw away a carefully sculpted career, *and* her parents' security, and ignore the stacks of work that came into the suite while she was tending the shop.

Even though Clarisse, the young mother who helped part-time, shared some duties, such as displays and sales, Leigh was the manager and responsible for the shop. In addition to that, she still continued some ongoing sales accounts for Bella. She had enough on her plate without Jarek and yet thoughts of him overlaid all others.

She picked up the pink-and-red pareu, the one that had looked so savagely beautiful as Jarek lay sprawled across it. She saw him again on the bed, the fringes against his tanned skin as he stared at her. He had caressed the fringes as he had touched her, those big broad hands light and skillful.

As a total package, Jarek was dark, powerful, brooding, wanting everything.

The fringes ran silkily through her fingers. Didn't she want everything? And this time, for herself?

Could she dare risk all that she had built, everyone who depended on her?

Jarek was working now, trying to fill a rush order for a tourist whose wife had loved the Stepanov furniture in their room. Leigh studied Deadman's Rock and the rising tide. She wondered what went wrong that day and why Annabelle had died. In a small motorboat, on a calm day, the passage should have been easy. What had Annabelle been thinking?

She seemed always to loom around Jarek, in those quiet moments when he looked toward Strawberry Hill.

Leigh wanted to hold Jarek, not with passion, but from danger. On impulse, she slung the pareu around her shoulders, covering her simple black sleeveless dress, and hurried from the Amoteh.

She wanted the fresh air blowing in her hair, the sun warming her, the feeling that she was alive and strong enough to face anything. She walked down the steps to the tourist pier, wandering past the various stalls, stopping to admire a vendor's display—sterling jewelry, seashells from the tropics, tropical shifts and woven sandals, the fried Chinese noodles, and beautiful flowers stacked in front of one stall, bouquets bunched by color. Various artists showed their canvases, intent upon painting at their easels.

Leigh watched a little boy earnestly tug his parents to a stall filled with wooden toy sailboats. While watching a small tourist boat ease back to its mooring, the passengers unload and walk up the ramp and steps to the wharf, she breathed the scents of ocean saltwater, fast food, flowers, happiness and life.

She felt alive, aware of every scent, every color, the breeze on her skin. Leigh closed her eyes, taking the beauty of just living into her, storing it.

When she opened her eyes again, Lars Anders loomed over her. He grabbed her bare arm roughly and shoved his sneer down close to her face. "So you sent Jarek to collect your money, did you? I might have known not to trust you, you slut."

Taken by surprise and disgusted by the alcohol on Lars's breath, Leigh stepped back. "What?"

"If you want him safe, you come to my place and make me happy."

She knew that Jarek had won the last brawl, but she feared that Lars might start another. "Leave me alone, unless you want real trouble. I won't hesitate to call the police."

"Oh, a tigress, huh? Maybe Jarek doesn't know how to handle a real woman, but I do. And I know what bad publicity can do to a business. You want trouble? I can give you that."

Leigh tugged her arm away, furious with his advance. She briskly rubbed the tender flesh of her inner arm where he had gripped her painfully. "Don't you ever come near me again."

His leer said he would.

She hurried away from him and at the end of the wharf found Ryan sitting hunched down, and looking at the waves. His T-shirt was stained and torn, his jeans as bad. "Ryan?"

He didn't look at her. "I hate this," he said flatly. "I should be out practicing for competition. Instead—yesterday they worked me like a slave, and then for relaxation, I hoed the garden for Bliss. After that, it was fixing the porch boards and putting up some dumb flower trellis. Then back up at the shop at seven, breaking my back. I get to have a little fresh air to wipe out the fumes, I guess. Then we're working overtime tonight. Some dumb rush order. I get overtime. Big deal. I'm going to die here and it's your fault. Maybe a saw will take off my hand and then gee, won't that be cool trying to get up on a board then?''

He turned to glare at her, the petulant little brother she'd always known. He looked tired and more lean, and she worried that perhaps he was working too hard. Ryan hadn't held a straight job and the transition from carefree to responsible might take time. When Ryan was in this mood, he usually didn't stay—and that would hurt Ed and Bliss. "I think you can do it, Ryan. You promised. Now I want your promise that you won't—"

She turned to see Jarek watching them, his thumbs hooked in his pocket, his legs braced.

"The master calls," Ryan muttered, rising to his feet. He stared darkly at her. "You look different. I'd think that with you in his bed, he'd go a little easy on your brother. You're not denying it, are you? You're actually sleeping with him. I see the way he looks at you. I'm a man. I know that look. But I always thought of you as being too busy for a love life.''

Leigh felt the blush creep up her cheeks. "That's none of your business.''

"Maybe I'll make it my business—if he doesn't treat you right. I don't want you hurt. You're too soft and vulnerable. You should be someone's wife by now and have a bunch of my nieces and nephews. This guy could mess you up bad. I wouldn't like that at all," Ryan stated before stalking off the pier and ignoring Jarek.

Suddenly a child laughingly escaped her parents on the pier. She cried out as she toppled off the board edge and tumbled into the dark water.

Everything happened at once—Ryan and Jarek running past Leigh, the tiny blond head bobbing in the ocean, the child's body still. With the rest of the crowd, Leigh ran after them, and watched her brother poise for the long dive.

Jarek's pose mirrored Ryan's, and then he stopped and drew back as Ryan shot like an arrow into the black swell and heart-beats later bobbed to the surface.

"Jarek, help him," Leigh pleaded. "Please—"

"He's doing fine. Let him do this."

But Leigh was already kicking off her sandals and Jarek's hard glance slashed at her. He grabbed the shawl around her shoulders and hauled her back against him with it. "Look at him swim, Leigh. He knows what he's doing. He needs this."

She ignored the tears flowing down her cheeks. "Jarek— do something," she whispered. "Let me go."

"No. Stay put." He glanced at the small ambulance van that was already prowling down the pier, lights flashing. Then Jarek climbed down a small ladder to a motorboat tied there. He revved the motor and headed toward Ryan. When the boat pulled close, Ryan hefted the small limp body up to Jarek's arms and then heaved himself up into the boat.

Ryan worked over the child as Jarek headed the small boat back to a wooden platform and the medics waiting there. Leigh tried to get past the crowd, edging closer to see as Ryan followed the medics and the child's parents inside the van. With lights flashing, it drove toward the small clinic nearby.

One of the crowd nearest the ambulance called back to the others on the pier, "She's alive! I heard the medics say the kid did a good job. She's breathing!"

In the setting sun, Jarek walked to her, his expression grim. Still wrapped in fear, still seeing Ryan's body arcing into the swells, Leigh's taut nerves reacted immediately. The shocking torrent of words that came from her were borne of fear and frustration, an after-release of emotions held too tightly from her encounters with Lars and the unhappy Ryan.

Did everyone know that she was sharing Jarek's bed? What would people think? Morris had trusted her to be discreet as always, and here she was, the focus of gossip and uncertain about her life and Jarek.

Jarek crossed his arms and studied her quietly. He knew her too well. Better than she knew herself at times—and that terrified her, too.

Instinctively she struck out at him, the after-reaction of terror. She knew the words stemmed from fear, but she couldn't stop them. Unreasonable and furious, they churned out of her. "You should have let me go. Don't ever stop me from helping my family again. What do you mean, he needed that? How could anyone need to do that terrifying dive? What if he needed me to help him? How could you stop me from helping him? Were you afraid?"

She'd battled for her family her entire life and now, shaken by Ryan's dive, she couldn't stop. Her encounter with Lars was still fresh and raw and she hurled that at Jarek, too. "And exactly where is the money I gave Lars? I understand you have it. You cannot just *do* things that affect me, Jarek. I have my pride, too, and I take care of my own. You've undermined my control over my life. And you're working Ryan too hard. He'll take off and Ed and Bliss will be hurt."

The statements were wild, accusatory, and even as Leigh hurled them at him, she knew they were wrong—that they came from somewhere deep inside her, to conceal the real depth of her emotions. She hadn't had such wild, fierce emotions or the need to control them—until now, when they were controlling her, shocking her.

Jarek's face lacked expression, his lips firmly pressed together, that ridge of muscle tensing in his throat. He slowly removed bills from his wallet and gave them to her.

Then he turned and walked away from her, his back rigid.

Leigh shook, stunned and horrified by her wild accusations, the terror that Ryan might have drowned still wrapped around her. Whatever she and Jarek had, it was now dead. As cold as she felt inside.

She held her head high, ignoring Lars's sneer as she passed. He'd seen everything, the ugliness erupt in her and Jarek's chilling reaction.

A woman who wanted to show off how pretty her little girl looked in a Bella ruffled-bottom gingham bathing suit blocked Leigh's passage up the steps. Forcing herself to be enthusiastic for the little girl's sake, Leigh took time to admire her. She managed a few steps away and an elderly woman with a cane asked her assistance down the steps. Taking care, Leigh gently helped her down the steps and firmly refused to take the money offered by the woman.

Then again, just midway up the steps, she couldn't refuse a small boy's shout to return his ball, just yards from the steps.

She finally managed to hurry into the Seawind Suite, locking the door behind her. Battered by the earlier scene, by the Leigh she didn't know, the shadowy room was momentarily safe. She hurled the pareu away and rubbed her hands over her face as she kicked off her sandals.

Leigh was horrified at how she had reacted, the accusations she had thrown at Jarek, the way he looked—cold and distant, as if he'd never—

She brushed away the tears with her hands. Working too hard, making love too much, and being too tired, shouldn't have caused that furious reaction—as though every problem she brooded and had withheld, even from herself, had thrust into the salt air between them. Unused to handling so many personal emotions, she knew exactly how to act when *other* people were affected—not herself. The stormburst was as if everything had torn out of her at once—her personal fears and doubts about herself as a woman in control of her life.

As a fax purred out of the machine, Leigh tried to think that it was better this way—the end, clean-cut and final. They were not a match, she reasoned as she glanced at the fax and saw once again Jarek's cold, rigid expression.

Come live with me....

Was she so afraid of sharing herself? And her heart?

She had to apologize to Jarek. But not right now, not when she was still shaking from reaction…not when she didn't understand her own mind and heart. She could say the wrong thing, upsetting him more. She tried for logic and failed. She had to apologize—Jarek didn't deserve any of the accusations she had thrown at him.

Then the shadows stirred, and Jarek quietly rose from a chair. "What was all that about?"

She should have expected him; Jarek was unpredictable. She wanted to go to him, to have him hold her amid the storm of her emotions. She needed desperately to hold him, to have those arms enfold her, to know that she hadn't lost him, hadn't destroyed what ran so strongly between them.

Instead she stood still, trying not to shake in the aftermath of what she had done. "Everything is happening too fast. I can't explain it, but I'm sorry. I apologize."

Jarek nodded slowly, watching her. "Ryan is just making adjustments in his life. He's older than most who start to become a responsible man and maybe it is harder on him. He's not working too hard, no more or less than any of us."

Leigh rubbed her arms, her body and heart chilled by her shocking reaction. "I know. That was sheer reaction on my part. I've just always managed the difficult parts of his life."

She shook her head, unable to look at Jarek, ashamed of her anger. "I'm so sorry. I really can't explain how horrible I acted."

The telephone rang and after a moment's hesitation, Leigh reached for it. Ryan quickly explained that the little girl was doing well, that everyone thought he was a hero. She'd never heard that sound of pride in his voice, and remembered Jarek's "He needs this."

She replaced the telephone. "The girl is doing fine."

Ryan was more than fine, he was bursting with pride and happiness. The incident was going to be in the local paper and he'd just turned down a hefty amount of money from the parents. He didn't think it was right to take money for acting as any man should.

She couldn't speak, searching Jarek's face for the anger she'd expected.

"I wouldn't have kept that money." The dark edge of his nicked pride slashed at her. "And Ryan has dived off cliffs and in high-board competition. He's good. He knew what he was doing. And he's qualified for lifesaving, though he hasn't used it. There comes a time when a man must act as a man— you haven't let him.''

"I know. You did what you thought was right. But it wasn't right for me. I'm Ryan's sister, and I couldn't bear to think that— You and I are so different.''

"What else is there?''

For a moment, Lars's angry face swept before her, but she shook her head. She didn't want Jarek fighting Lars again, and he would, to defend her honor. To the Stepanovs, honor and pride were high priorities. "Nothing. Except that I know you weren't afraid. I can't imagine you as fearing anything.''

Jarek reached out a hand to wrap it around her wrist, tugging her against him. His green eyes narrowed down at her, as his thumb caressed her inner wrist and his other hand smoothed her hair. "You're afraid to live with me, aren't you? That's what this is all about. Maybe it's my fault then, for pushing too hard—for wanting you too much.''

He shrugged lightly, and his next statement was husky and uneven, as if it had been tugged from his heart. "What can I say, but that I am a Stepanov man who wants his woman very much? I make mistakes. For that, I am sorry.''

She hadn't expected that uncertainty, that humble admission. "I'm a package deal, Jarek. I can't see you taking on my family permanently, and I won't desert them. Summer will be over and the shop will be closed for the season—a few swimsuits will be left in the gift shop. Then I'll have to go back to work in my real capacity and relocate my parents.''

His head went back as though she had slapped him. His deepened accent said that he was disturbed. "I know that it is soon, but already I know there will be no end for us.''

"I have to think of my family. They need me.''

His blank expression said he didn't understand. Then his head went back with that arrogant tilt. "You would think that of me—that I would ask you to separate yourself from your family. Family is family. It stays together. So do lovers, so that they can whisper to each other in the night and share what bothers them—that and more. You leave me each morning and I wonder where you'll decide to stay that night. Is it wrong to want your clothes hanging next to mine, some small reassurance that you'll come back to me?'' he added more gently, smiling softly at her.

"I'm just trying to be sensible. Everything is happening so fast,'' she whispered, looking up at his tender expression.

The tip of his finger ran down her nose in a light tease. "What don't you trust? This heat—this hunger between us? Or the deeper one, that burns inside me now, the need to hold you and keep you safe, to comfort you when you are weary and troubled, to lie at your side each night.''

"We've only known each other for a short time, Jarek. It's taken me a lifetime to structure a life from that of a gypsy to some measure of security.''

"True. But we know each other in what counts. That you make me happy. That sometimes—when you're not thinking too much—I make you happy. Maybe we can build from that? Mmm?'' he asked as he brushed his lips across hers.

She shivered, a reaction caused by her swing from confused emotions to focusing upon Jarek's beguiling smile. "I'll try not to push too much. You try not to think too much, okay? Stop worrying.''

"Go with the flow?'' she asked, feeling lighter and happier, just because Jarek was there, holding her, smiling down at her.

"If we can do that together,'' he whispered, and settled in to kiss her with the hunger that grew until Leigh forgot everything else.

She arched up to him, and Jarek skimmed her body, his hands going low, then lifting her one-piece, matte, jersey dress from her. There was that quick, dark look of possession, the flaring of his nostrils. He nuzzled her cheek, nipped her earlobe lightly and began a downward path to her breasts.

"You smell so good,'' he whispered roughly, his hands cupping her bottom, easing away her panties, his fingers trailing delicately upward, tantalizing. "That woman scent. You're already so hot—"

Hot? She was burning, aching, her body needing him fully against her. "You can't win all the arguments like this…." she managed to say before the first sensual jolt hit her. Then, "Hurry—"

Jarek lifted her and carried her to the sprawling bed, tossing her lightly upon it. In the next instant, he was above her, in her, taking, just as she was giving. His mouth tugged at her breasts, licked, nibbled and the fever took her higher, the cords tightening unbearably within her. Just then, at the climax, Jarek looked down at her, his expression almost savage. "You give everything. You take everything. That is how it should be."

She felt just as primitive, surging up to tighten around him, taking what she wanted, enjoying, reveling in being a part of Jarek's body, lock and key. Urgent and furious, the tiny explosions racked her, staking her beneath him.

When Leigh surfaced drowsily, Jarek's hands smoothing her belly and her sensitive breasts, she found that wistful expression again. A smug smile wiped it away.

"I've been zapped," she whispered lazily and tried to lift her head. She couldn't.

He chuckled at that and kissed her forehead. "Have to go. We're loading furniture into a truck for delivery tomorrow and finishing some special orders. I'll be lucky if I can stand now, let alone work."

Now, that smug smile was hers. It stayed when Jarek dressed and reached to pull the sheet over her. He leaned over her to nuzzle her neck. "You're too tempting, love. We need time."

She glanced at the bedside clock. "That took all of twenty minutes."

His hand eased under her to cup her breast. "Mmm. You were rushing me. I couldn't resist. I'll see you tonight, love."

"Don't be so certain of yourself. I just might be busy."

Jarek flipped her over and swooped in for a hard hungry kiss. "Oh, you will be. I promise."

As if he wanted to imprint how she looked in his arms, Jarek's gaze wandered down her body, taking in her shoulders, her breasts—

He frowned and bent to study the dark bruises on her upper arm, the clear impressions of individual fingers. He lifted her arm to kiss the bruises. "I'm too rough with you. I'm sorry," he whispered so humbly that she could have cried.

She couldn't tell him of her encounter with Lars, or of his lewd suggestion. She didn't want Jarek endangered again.

Leigh framed his face with her hands. "You made love to me, that's all. I wanted you as desperately."

"I mishandled you. I'm sorry, love." Clearly disturbed, Jarek eased from her. He stared out the window to the rock lurking in the distance, and Leigh knew that he was thinking of another woman.

To distract him from Annabelle's whispers, Leigh threw away the sheet and rose to her feet. "Too bad you're not taking a shower with me—there's plenty of room. But you have all that overtime to do tonight, don't you?"

I'm alive, Annabelle, and he's mine now. You can't have him.

Jarek's grin said he admired the picture Leigh made as she attempted to be seductive. Television commercials were wonderful courses, she thought as she twisted her finger in her hair and licked her lips. She lowered her lids and served him a sultry stare.

"I remember that pose from your parents' albums," Jarek said thoughtfully. "You were six, nude and sleepy."

"I'm working on a project here, Jarek. Be cooperative."

He grinned at her and started walking toward her. "How cooperative?"

Uncertain that she could withstand another passionate round without completely coming undone, Leigh shrieked and stepped into the bathroom, closing the door behind her.

She heard Jarek chuckle and then she smiled to the well-loved, happy woman in the mirror. Later, she held that smile as she settled down to work at her desk.

When Jarek got back to the shop, Fadey was grinning. "Tell her you love her."

"It's too soon. She's scared now."

Fadey's grin widened. "Tell her you think of the babies she will give you. Oh, I am not so old that I don't know how it is when a man wants a woman, when he thinks nothing of her, and puts the wrong finish on good wood. You don't make mistakes, my son, but the customer ordered rubbed finish, not the one you chose. I already called them. The woman was eager to take a good discount price."

Surprised, Jarek swung to study the tall narrow chest, a special order to fit a narrow wall space. Trained in finishes and checking them before applying, he'd made a crucial mistake with a custom piece.

In his passion, he'd handled Leigh roughly. To a Stepanov man, that was unforgivable.

Nine

Still disturbed by his rough handling of Leigh, Jarek worked quietly, rubbing another layer of finish to the bedroom set. In the bald, bold lights of the shop, the wood gleamed. The windows were open, carefully screened against insects as a fan gently blew away the fumes.

With each stroke of his rag, Jarek thought of Leigh's smooth skin, the darkening marks of his fingers. He wished he could remove the bruises as easily as he could smooth away an unfortunate scratch on the wood.

The small red stripes her nails had made on his back had quickly faded, and they were dear to him, marks of her passion.

How could he ask her to live with him and not touch her? How could he live with himself, if he hurt her in his passion?

The shop was blaring with boisterous Russian accordion music. A distance away from where finish was carefully applied, Fadey's saw was ripping through wood. Ryan had returned to the shop, though he could have stayed away. With earphones firmly in place and a cassette player attached to his belt, he was focused on the intricacies of wood glue, dowels and bench clamps. His head bobbed in a different rhythm than the Russian music's beat. Periodically he looked dreamily at the "blank," leaning unshaped against the wall. From the layers of foam and wood, he would make his first surfboard—when rush season slowed a bit.

Mikhail had chosen to work in the shop that night. Preferring his sons at his side, Fadey had given the other men extra pay, and sent them home.

Jarek glanced at his brother, who was now leaning back against the workbench, staring at the sawdust on the rough wooden floor. Mikhail held a slice of his mother's black bread in his hand. Without his suit and wearing a fair amount of sawdust and sweat, Mikhail didn't resemble the laird of Amoteh Resort. He looked like any other Stepanov male—tough, proud and a bit savage beneath the layers of civilization.

When Mikhail looked up, he scowled at Jarek and spoke of the one person who could get beneath his tough veneer, though he wouldn't let her know it. "Ellie Lathrop is a spoiled brat. If she weren't the owner's daughter, she'd be persona non grata at the Amoteh."

He tore off a chunk of bread and chewed it, clearly irritated. "She's been a pain since I started working for Mignon International. She has no concept of working, or consideration for people who do. In fact, I see no reason why I should accommodate her on a moment's notice—hell, no, I'm not having her redecorate a room with a children's decor at the Amoteh. The staff is busy enough with scheduled events, let alone something Ellie just dreams up on the spur of the moment."

If there was one person who could make Mikhail shed his cool exterior—if only in front of his family—it was Ellie Lathrop. Their run-ins were legendary—Ellie fearless when facing Mikhail and just as determined to get her way as he was in thwarting her.

Jarek privately enjoyed seeing Mikhail on a collision course with Ellie. The woman was strong-minded and took a mile when an inch was offered. And she disturbed Mikhail more than he would admit.

At times, Jarek decided, older brothers needed to be reminded that they were not quite invincible—it kept them human. "You've done it before."

"Not this time. Her father is a good businessman. We may argue over ethics at times, but I respect what he's built. Paul Lathrop came from the streets and he created a worldwide chain of resorts. But I will not have a spoiled jet-setter, unemployed, wealthy, pampered woman disrupting the Amoteh's staff. All the painting has been done for the season, barring incidents. The golf course is the priority now. We've got a celebrity tournament coming up."

He lifted the lid to the large casserole dish and bent to sniff the beef mixture. For the moment, Ellie was dismissed in lieu of good food. "Mmm. Mom's stroganoff."

Fadey switched off the saw and washed his hands. He turned off the passionate Russian folk music and grinned at the meal Mary Jo had brought earlier to the shop. "And gingerbread cookies with jam in them, like my mother made in the old country. My wife knows how hard I work…and she is glad she is not here, but that our sons help me—and Ryan, too."

He reached to lift Ryan's earphones and a blast of reggae music filled the now quiet shop. Fadey shook his head. "So sad. It's not music to stir the blood. Let's eat."

The men ate in silence and then the shop's door creaked open, framing Leigh, dressed in a T-shirt and sweatpants. A red ribbon held her curls back from her face, and Jarek remembered painfully how pale and worried she had looked when he saw the bruise—as if she were afraid he would do it again.

Jarek's chest tightened. *He would die before hurting her.*

"Ah, my little girl," Fadey exclaimed, motioning her to them at the workbench. "Come…sit…eat. Then we work.

When this rush is done, and you have time, you come to Fadey's house and learn how to make tea, the *zavarka*, eh?''

After his bear hug, which lifted her feet off the floor, he patted the red bow on top of her head. ''Pretty.''

''I hope I'm not disturbing you.'' Leigh's glance at Jarek was wary.

He could only take her hand and kiss it, and let his eyes apologize for causing her pain. The bruises on her arm mocked him, and he felt shame at how he had treated a woman he had invited into his life and home.

Later as they worked, Jarek glanced at Leigh. From her worried looks at him, he sensed that she had come to tell him something important—like ''Get out of my life. It's over.''

He didn't blame her; a woman wouldn't want a man who hurt her. Intent upon his thoughts, he didn't notice her going into the store room for clean rags.

Then he saw the door to his past was open, the memories he had storied away of Annabelle. In the bald light, Leigh stood holding the tarp as she looked at the cradle and its jumbled contents. She'd discovered his memories and his heartbreak.

He came to stand beside her, uncertain as to what he could say. Then, as if sharing the past and his pain, Leigh turned to hold him tightly. ''You didn't hurt me, Jarek. And you're not responsible for Annabelle's death,'' she whispered.

Jarek smoothed her arms. ''For me to hurt you is unthinkable.''

She drew back and shook him slightly. ''I told you, you didn't. Don't you dare back off from me. Don't you dare withhold what you feel from me, not about this.''

''If you look at these things and feel pity for me, I couldn't stand it.'' That fear jumped alive and quivering within him—that she should pity him. She'd obviously come tonight to reassure him. Was he really that fragile? Could she see inside him so clearly?

''Maybe you should look at them again—take a fresh look

with the years putting distance between what happened. You might understand more now than you did when you were fresh with grief. You can tell me about her. Maybe that will help. But you haven't let her go, rather you haven't let your guilt go. I don't believe in ghosts, but she's definitely still in you. The other night, you had a nightmare and cried out her name. I think…I think that I like it better when you say my name, especially when we're…ah…together."

He took her hands and raised them to his lips. Leigh saw too deeply into him and he wasn't certain if he liked her examining his fears, or his guilt. And he had spread them before her, stark and painful. His passions, yes, of course—she should have that part of him. But he was uneasy about the softer elements that ran like a current through him, nagging…. "Come home with me tonight."

She nodded toward the cradle filled with photographs and mementos. "Bring these. I want to know the woman you loved."

"She believed in the Hawaiian's curse. Maybe it's true." Jarek looked out to the night, where the moths were beating against the screens, trying to come to the shop lights. "Is it so important?"

"I think so. I want to understand her."

Just touching Leigh, placing his forehead against hers helped. "Sometimes there was no understanding her—or myself. I should have done something. I didn't—Annabelle is dead now."

"But you're not and neither am I. I want to help." Leigh smoothed his brow with her fingertips, and as they traced his face, Jarek felt an easing of that tight corner he never wanted to examine. But now Leigh was in his heart, too. Jarek drew her against him, and buried his face in those fragrant curls.

"Your parents chose the right name," he whispered, thinking how precious she was to him.

At Jarek's house later, after a long sensuous shower, Leigh sat by his side as he opened the old albums. One by one the pictures of Annabelle revealed her raven beauty, that elegant photogenic face—and Jarek's love for her. The two young sweethearts had sailed together, grinning at the camera, then the newly married couple kissed on the steps of Amoteh's small church. Jarek had carried her over the threshold of their new home.

Then later, Annabelle's private haunting began to show on their faces, and the glow that had surrounded them earlier had faded. While a tense but smiling Jarek stood at her side, Annabelle seemed worried and focused on something else—was it her destiny with Kamakani?

"She believed in that damn curse, was obsessed with it," Jarek stated suddenly, harshly, as though he were remembering all at once the scenes that had led to Annabelle's death.

"You could have protected her from all else, but herself," Leigh noted softly, aching for him.

Battling with the past, seeing it with a fresh view and Leigh's help, Jarek paced the length of his house. He shook his head and slammed his fist onto the counter, rattling the dishes stacked there. "She said she would rather die than go on without a baby. I thought we should adopt, but Annabelle couldn't allow that—she thought all that she was as a woman rested in if she could conceive. She only wanted me that one time, to give her a baby. We—"

Jarek's tall body shook with emotion, his face strained, his fists at his side. "I'd forgotten some of this—the dark side of what happened. We didn't make love anymore—unless it was on demand, when it was her time to conceive—that was just before the second miscarriage. When Annabelle wanted something, she was obsessed and there was no reasoning with her. She was on pills, edgy, and fascinated by Kamakani. I couldn't get her to see reason, that it was only a legend.... I tried to get her to agree to counseling for us both."

He held his breath, releasing it harshly as if he'd kept silent on one thought for years. "I think—I think she was in love with him. The way she talked about him—"

"I don't think any of this was about you—it was about her. From what you say, I don't think a baby would have given her all she needed. Or you, for that matter."

Jarek stared at her, his expression haunted. Then he walked out to sit on the front steps. Leigh came to sit beside him, her arm around him, her head on his shoulder.

"How do you know so much?" he whispered rawly, leaning to kiss her forehead.

She thought of all the times that Bliss had told her to feel with her heart, not tempered by her mind. "Let her go, Jarek. Please."

"I am trying. You were right—time did put some logic into what happened." His kiss brushed her cheeks and tasted her lips, once and again, softly, tenderly. Then as if he were starting a new beginning, Jarek stood and without a word bent to lift Leigh into his arms.

They made love silently, sweetly. As if they were floating in sunshine, each touch lingered magically.

And long into the night, Leigh held him as he slept heavily. She should have told him that he wasn't responsible for her bruises—that Lars had called her suite today, and his words weren't sweet. But Jarek had enough on his mind, placing Annabelle into the past, and Leigh wouldn't have him endangered.

She would be very careful and Lars would tire of his cat-and-mouse game. Then Jarek stirred in her arms, his hands skimming her body, his body already hard and nudging her hip.

Leigh gave him everything, the heat and the passion she'd saved all her life—just for him. She opened herself to the deepest, fullest hunger, giving and taking. She took pleasure inside her, hoarded it, and returned it to him in the wild storm.

She gave him everything—but truth. He hadn't hurt her, Lars had.

Jarek grinned at Leigh as she struggled, pinned beneath him on the beach blanket as the driftwood fire lit the mid-July night. She shrieked with laughter as he tickled her, then bent to lift up her T-shirt and push his head beneath it, playfully nuzzling her breasts.

He tugged the front bikini bow with his teeth, swept his hand down Leigh's squirming legs and opened her jeans. The sound of her laughter, freed to the night, caught him as he nuzzled her stomach.

"I'll get you—" she cried out breathlessly as Jarek suddenly rolled to his back, taking Leigh over him.

"Mmm. Threats. Let's just see if you can. Get creative." Maybe, just maybe, with Leigh poised over him, he felt young and carefree again. Maybe he felt as if he were starting life all over.

They slept in his bed every night, playing when they could, but Leigh still returned to her suite in the mornings.

He allowed himself a well-pleased smirk. He wasn't alone in enjoying their time together, whether it was Leigh riding behind him on the motorcycle, or rummaging in the shops for some keepsake to exclaim over, or chasing and teasing each other in the summer nights. Leigh's laughter said she had relaxed, that she trusted him. She seemed to be uncoiling from that tight business knot, to enjoy each breath of fresh air, the excitement of the days—and nights. They each worked hard, and yet came together with a surprising passion.

Leigh flopped to her back, watching the stars overhead. "Tell me about them. Tell me how you were when you and Mikhail and your parents would sail, setting course by them."

Jarek lay by her side, taking her hand. "Well, there is the North Star—"

As he explained, Leigh placed her head on his shoulder, and when he was finished, his private course charted, Jarek turned to her. He'd given her time, letting her feel her way through their relationship. "Come live with me."

"I can't. Morris—"

The name nettled and Jarek jackknifed into sitting, staring

at the fire. Slowly Leigh eased to sit beside him. "I don't know anything about running a household, Jarek. I grew up in a van, remember?"

"Do you think I want a housekeeper?" he asked, more savagely than he wanted as he turned to look at her. Over his shoulder, Jarek's expression pinned her. "The question is, what do you want?"

"You," she whispered after a heartbeat. If ever she wanted to be selfish, to take what she wanted, it was Jarek.

"Show me." The command was arrogantly male, typical Stepanov.

Leigh considered the challenge. She knew what she wanted, and she would make certain Jarek knew, too. But she wouldn't be ordered by him on the when, where and how. Setting her terms, Leigh rose slowly, and walked slowly away from the beach bonfire toward his house.

Inside the neat single room house, she undressed slowly and turned to face Jarek as he entered.

She recognized the dark edge of his temper and his uncertainty, and her own. He closed the door with a little more force than necessary, leaning back against it. Jarek—tall, dark, arrogant, distant. Those beautiful sea-green eyes were shadowed, glittering, as he considered her. "You love me, of course. Or you wouldn't give yourself to me. I know you too well, even in this short time. You're meticulous about releasing yourself into someone else's care. And you definitely do release yourself in my arms, in your passion."

That bald statement, so typical of him, brought warmth to Leigh's cheeks, but she wasn't getting waylaid from holding her own with him.

"Of course, I love you. But don't expect any favors because of that minor fact. You're pushy, Jarek. I make my own decisions."

"Then," he stated slowly, carefully defining what ran between them. His tone was sheer male pride and arrogance. "In this, you think of what you want first. You want me."

His verbal smirk was arrogant—and true. In the shadows, his expression softened, and he ran his hand over his chest, rubbing it. The thoughtful, sensual gesture slammed into Leigh, taking away her breath. She knew how those hands felt on her, what magic they could do....

She braced herself against the force of Jarek's attraction. He knew she was susceptible to that dark look, taking in the curves of her body. She could almost feel his lips against her skin, that electricity streaking beneath it. She could feel them tug gently at her breasts, the erotic flick of his tongue. She could feel those calloused broad hands, so certain where and how to pleasure her.

"Come to me," she ordered quietly, matching his arrogance with her own. To have her, Jarek would have to cross the space between them, a silent admission she had to have.

His head tilted with just that slight warning of a man who didn't take orders lightly. "You said you love me."

Leigh nodded slowly and realized that this was the first time she'd tested his need for her. Games? Maybe. But then she was a woman, enjoying a man, and the part of seductress excited her. She wanted this intimacy for herself, the woman, not the machine concerned and functioning for everyone else. *With Jarek, she was absolutely greedy, and that frightened her. Yet she would hold her course—*

"Do you question me in that?" she served him the challenge in the old-fashioned language he used when deeply touched. It was now her language, that of a woman in love, but not obedient. A woman who took what she wanted.

She was honest with Jarek in her emotions. She laughed when her heart felt full of sunshine with him. She was quiet when words were not needed to share a simple pleasure—such as the big fiery sun seeming to sink into the ocean.

She hadn't told him of Lars's continuing lewd remarks. Jarek was a man to take care of business and from his expression now as he tossed away his T-shirt, she was very much on his mind. Leigh pushed images of Lars into the night outside where he belonged; she would not have Jarek hurt again.

"Take off the rest," she whispered, even as her legs weakened at that gleaming, powerful chest, the muscles surging on his arms, that flat, rippled belly.

Watching her, Jarek slowly kicked off his canvas shoes. He unsnapped his jeans and they sagged slightly as he walked toward her. "Take them off yourself."

She knew what waited for her when he looked at her like that. She recognized the leap of her pulse, the softening, warming dampness of her body, ready for him. She felt the ache in her breasts, the fire leaping beneath her skin, the hunger that stalked her. The game between them took too long. Leigh couldn't wait any longer, despite her promise to herself.

She'd told him she loved him. It wasn't easy for her to leave the safe world for Jarek, but she had.

And now she wanted him. Then. There.

"Ohhh!" She recognized the sound of frustration, of desire and hunger in her voice. She took the last step, bringing their bodies together. Jarek's hands found her hips, locking on to them, a sensual, primitive claiming. His caress slid up to her waist, then higher to cup her breasts, and that dark flickering look said lovemaking this time would be a voyage, enriched by her admission of love.

Had he been so uncertain of her?

She should have told him about Lars—

But then Jarek was bending to take her mouth hungrily and she stopped thinking—only feeling, his body against hers, carrying her quickly away to a place only they shared.

He came into her smoothly, filling her, arching her hips to him, watching her, his eyes glittering in the night. "Say it again. Now. Say you love me."

His hands ran down her thighs, smoothing them, then coursed a true path up to her breasts. He could be fierce, relentless, primitive—but then, now, so was she.

Leigh met that first hard possessive kiss with her own needs. Open. Scorching. Pure temptation to do as he wanted.

But she broke away, breathless, trembling with the pleasure already consuming them. Breathing hard, she flattened against the bed, fingers digging into his shoulders. She could be just as demanding, just as arrogant, pleased that they were matched so well. "And you love me, of course."

"Of course. I would not be so sweet and pleasant, obeying your commands, if I didn't." His mouth curved slightly. "Enjoying yourself?"

"Of course."

As Jarek studied her beneath him, his expression closed, darkened and there was that slow flickering look down their joined bodies.

Leigh's senses prickled, tiny jolts of a need so primitive she couldn't understand it pounded at her. Deep inside, it warmed and curled and hungered. "What are you thinking of—when you do that? Look at us together?"

Jarek's eyes traveled slowly up her body, pale against his. He moved slowly, deeply, watching her meet him in an easy rhythm, watching her face. "You're so warm, Leigh. Your skin gives off this incredible scent. And you're biting your lip, a sign that you're fighting going over the edge—but you're so lovely when you ignite—"

She cried out as he moved, gently rubbing his chest against her breasts, then taking the peaks into his mouth, treating them gently. "You're burning now."

"So are you," she managed to say unevenly, and smoothed Jarek's broad back, the muscles sliding beneath that wonderful skin. She skimmed her hands over his chest, toying with his nipples, treating them as he had done to her. "You're shaking."

"It's a powerful feeling, to be inside the woman I love, thinking of what it could mean, that I could give you a child like this. That you would hold a part of me inside you, cherishing and nourishing him."

She should have expected Jarek's thought, because reverence for family and children ran deep within him. He would want his own child from her. The shattering image slammed into her, and then she recognized that emotion running deep within her, unlabeled and fierce—that of wanting that tiny piece of the man she loved. Every instinct in her warmed and softened, her hand caressing his face as he smoothed her damp curls back from her face. Amid the storm, one that started as a challenge, the softness came prowling, something just as strong and fierce as what ran between them, but new and fresh and cherished.

There would be other times to consider this new intimacy, sharing softness and dreams amid the passion, but for now, with Jarek's hard mouth prowling hers, tormenting her—

Leigh dived into the pleasure, the tightening of her body, the heat surging through them, devouring them.

The pleasure contracted once and again, tossing her against him feverishly. She held him tightly, aware that in her pleasure she had nipped his shoulder, that the sound of his harsh breathing excited her as much as his body moving against her, strong, fierce—just as she wanted.

Jarek caught her on that first hard peak, held her there, soared with her, over and over.

Leigh gradually floated lightly down from their passion, smiling drowsily as Jarek's heart slowed its race. He came into her care slowly, letting her soothe him, his face resting against her throat.

"Leigh...." He sighed, and the name on his lips was hers, not another woman who had held him too long in darkness.

She gripped his hair and tugged his head back gently. "Say it again. Say my name."

There was that arrogance, a male unwilling to be commanded, that lifted brow, challenging her. "Say mine."

"Ohh!"

Jarek grinned, obviously delighted. "I love it when you're fierce, Precious. In fact, I love you any way I can get you."

"I'll show you fierce," she promised and Jarek chuckled as she moved over him.

In the morning, Leigh awoke with Jarek spooned to her back, his hands already doing their magic. "I love that woman scent. It's arousing. But then, it's the scent of the woman I love."

She smiled dreamily as his face nuzzled her throat. "You're always aroused."

"You have that affect." His hands were smoothing her thighs now, moving upward—

She slowly moved her body in rhythm to his caresses, floating in pleasure. "Mmm. What time is it?"

Jarek sighed slowly. "Almost six-thirty."

Leigh came wide-awake. "Six-thirty? Morris is coming this morning. I've got to—"

"Yes, you do. But here's something to take with you," Jarek murmured as he turned her and dived in for that first, hot hungry kiss.

As if rekindled, waiting, simmering from the last time they made love, she ignited.

Twenty-five minutes later, Leigh lay on her back unable to move, every muscle drained and sated. Jarek lay beside her, toying with her hair.

She turned to him. "You deliberately wasted me. I've been zapped again. No warning, just plain zapped."

"It appears it was a mutual zapping."

There was a tenseness she didn't understand lurking in the shadows, something dark and brooding about Jarek. She hurried to dress, picking up her clothing from the floor, while Jarek slipped into his jeans. He went to the kitchenette and started making coffee, but his expression had closed again.

She needed to hurry—

Leigh stopped at the door. She needed to understand what bothered Jarek. "What's wrong?"

"I love you, of course. You love me. I'm jealous. I don't

like it. I don't like the thought of my woman hurrying off to meet another man.''

Leigh pushed her hand through her mussed hair. She didn't have time—

Yes, she did. For once, Leigh placed business needs aside. Jarek was more important than anything else. "I'll cancel."

"No, you won't. It is my problem. You are a business-woman. I know you need this contract to work out well. So, I am selfish. I know it. Go on.''

Leigh went to him, taking his face in her hands and trailing a flurry of kisses over the rugged planes. "I do love you, Jarek. I just don't know how to deal with everything just yet. I'm not used to taking what I want, for myself, either.''

He kissed her palm. "Dinner tonight?"

"I can't. I— Jarek, please come to dinner with us. I want you to meet Morris. He's been so kind to me and we've planned to dine with Mikhail at the resort.''

He nodded slowly, that devastating smile just for her. "You'll think about me, of course. Today, when you can.''

Beneath the arrogance was the vulnerability Leigh knew needed tending. "Of course. How could I not?''

Jarek reached for a long velvet box and opened it. "Wear this. I need to know that you wear something of mine. Will you?''

The ornate necklace, heavy and encrusted with semiprecious gems, obviously old and valuable, glittered across his broad palm. Jarek's look at her was shielded, as if he feared she would refuse. "She never wore it. I never offered. It is not the ring I want you to wear, but it will serve.''

Leigh's first impulse was to refuse the obvious family heir-loom, but Jarek's expression told her how much it would mean to him. Jarek had been badly hurt and he'd shielded his heart for years, but now he was offering it to her. When she nodded, he placed the heavy necklace around her throat.

"Wear it and think of me, just this day after you told me

you love me,'' he whispered, his open hand resting over the necklace. ''Think of wearing my ring. Think of marrying me.''

Morris's flight was canceled until the next day, and Leigh's panic eased; she had time to research and arrange the presentation to him. *The question was, what did she want? And what could she logically have?*

Logically, because she couldn't let go of the realities that her family depended on her.

The answer came back through the night. In the past, more than anything she'd wanted safety her entire life, and to know that her family was well and provided for. Now, she wanted that, but Jarek, too.

And he would want marriage and a family. *I love you, of course.*

The images of little untamed Jareks grinning up at her was almost frightening. Almost.

Rather, the idea fascinated her. Leigh hugged the take-out dinner that Georgia had prepared; she smiled at the stars as she hurried toward Jarek's house. There was an odd pleasure in taking dinner to Jarek, in surprising him when he thought she would be working late. She'd never thought of herself as a woman who would fetch for a lover, or someone who would enjoy surprises. Now she did both. But then, Jarek had prepared enough picnic and dinner meals for her. He seemed to enjoy caring for her—rubbing her tense shoulders after a hard day at paperwork, smoothing her temples, diverting her from a massive business problem with Bella—one in which she could do nothing just then.

If he were jealous, she was territorial, and not wanting to give Annabelle an inch to retrieve Jarek.

She needed him, too…to hear that deep uneven voice whisper those wonderful things to her.

In her telephone conference with Morris, he'd said that he was worried about her. ''You've changed, Leigh. I hear it in your voice. You've never been guarded with me before. Is something wrong?''

Despite her assurances, Morris was arriving tomorrow for a full overview of the pilot resort shop.

That bonus she needed for Ed and Bliss and Ryan dangled right in front of her. She'd always taken care of them, and now—

What did she want? What could she have?

After a day thinking of Jarek, of how he had pushed through old memories, trying to make sense of Annabelle's death, Leigh wasn't focused. She made mistakes in inventory and cash balancing, and she had been curt with Mikhail.

His silence and that one arched brow said the discussion about her outside display rack wasn't going any further. On the other hand, she sensed he was enjoying her distraction.

She also sensed that deep within that cool, distant exterior, Mikhail could be as passionate as Jarek or Fadey.

Leigh noted the light rain, the rising wind, but her thoughts were on Jarek. He'd opened his painful past to her and she knew that he was still rummaging through bits of it, placing it aside.

The Stepanov brothers were irritating, arrogant and too proud for their own good. They were moody, alternately cool and friendly, and just keeping up with both of them was enough to—

Leigh smiled tightly. Her one satisfaction with Mikhail was his obvious snit about Ellie Lathrop's demand of a suite's room decorated for a child. Today, while he was laying down his edict that the display rack should not be outside the shop, he was holding a teddy bear as if he could strangle it...or the woman who had sent it with other toys—Ellie.

The trail between the pines was sandy and easily seen in the moonlight. Leigh thought she saw something stir in the shadows and then Lars's beefy body loomed in front of her, blocking her path. "What do you have for me, honey?" he asked, leering at her.

For the first time, he frightened her. She'd been so confident that she could handle him—in the right circumstances.

But this was his chosen time and place, not hers. "Move out of my way."

He grabbed her arm, hauling her up close to him, and took the Amoteh's insulated dinner box from her. He dropped it onto the ground. "Thanks for the dinner."

She could smell alcohol on his breath as he jerked her closer, hurting her upper arms. "Let me go—"

"When I'm done—"

Then Jarek's face came out of the night, and Leigh shook at the violence in it.

"Let her go, Lars."

Lars shoved her away, and his knife glittered in the moonlight. Jarek bent and came up, his fist slamming into Lars's belly. His other hand gripped the man's wrist, twisting it. He took the knife and hurled it, point first into a tree.

While Lars bent over, trying to catch his breath, Jarek turned to Leigh. "Do you want him charged with assault, or do you want me to—?"

She feared what he would do and shook her head. "Neither. Just, please, take me home."

Jarek stood very still, his legs braced. He watched Lars slink into the shadows, making his way back toward the town.

"Whose home?" Jarek asked very quietly, and she knew the reckoning of the secret she'd kept from him would not be sweet.

Ten

Jarek methodically placed the roast chicken and pasta meal that Georgia had prepared onto the table. The ordinary, everyday task, lining the napkins carefully with the silverware, filling the water and wine glasses, gave him something to do when his emotions were shaken, tumbling through him.

Leigh was so much a part of him now—and she hadn't trusted him. She sat across the table from him; the candlelight flickered on her pale face and glittered on his family's necklace. Her hand on it, over her throat, was a protective gesture. *Did she think he would hurt her?*

Jarek sat back in his chair. "How long has Lars been bothering you?"

She looked at the untouched meal in her plate. "Several times since that day Ryan rescued that little girl. He's called, but a disconnect button is easy enough to push. I'm sorry that you thought the marks on my arm were yours...I told you they weren't. I know how much that bothered you, but I didn't want you hurt or hurting someone because of me."

For a moment, Jarek could not speak. "Those were *his* marks? He touched with that much force? And you didn't tell me?" Jarek's open hand slammed against the table, rattling the dishes there. "Do you have any idea what he could have done to you?"

When she refused to answer, he continued, "You can't push a disconnect button when a man is almost twice your size and drunk, and he's near you. *What were you thinking?*"

Those gold eyes lifted and darkened, the stirring of her temper whispered in the candlelight. "I've handled situations before. I didn't see the need to involve you."

"You love me, but you don't trust me to tell me something like this? You come to my bed every night, and you didn't tell me?" he demanded.

His fear for her ruled him, the image of Lars holding her prisoner, bending her body against his bulk—Jarek had been on his way to see her, and then suddenly in the moonlight he saw that blood-chilling scene. But deeper than his anger, was the painful knowledge that Leigh had been keeping an important secret from him.

"I didn't want you hurt." The statement was resentful and taut.

Jarek pushed back his pride and anger and realized that his words came out too cold. "'Hurt.' I'm a *man*, Leigh. I'm bigger, stronger, and I've been in a few fights. What makes you think *you* could protect *me*? Or that I would *want* you to? What do you think it does to me, to know that you didn't trust me?"

Leigh straightened and crossed her arms in front of her. "Back off. I did what I thought was right. Violence has never been a part of my life and I am not having it now."

Leigh's expression was rigid as she looked at him. "How long is this inquisition going to last? It's the first one I've ever had, so I'm not experienced."

"Then get experienced." He didn't mean to snap at her,

but fear, mixed with rage and pain battled within him. Would she take off his necklace? Would she leave him when she saw his primitive, raging side?

But then, he'd never been so angry, had he? A man had hurt her and she hadn't told him.

"What now? Is that the worst you've got?" Leigh invited calmly. "Yes, I do love you. And I think there will be times that I want to handle my life my way. I make mistakes, but I want to take care of the people I love. I need to. Don't blame me for being me, Jarek."

His emotions slowly eased. Leigh loved. She simply acted to protect him because she considered him to be her own.

That thought helped, but he wasn't done sulking. "I should have expected this, after you tried to buy him off."

"It was important to me to handle this situation, Jarek. But, if it happens again, I will tell you immediately—only if you promise me now that you will consider my thoughts on the matter. You can be very impetuous. I like caution. I've lived with impetuous people before—my parents—and I've tried for stability in my life. Except for you. You're swaggering, arrogant and passionate. I never know how your moods will turn. Still, here I am, aren't I?"

That concession salved, but he knew it had cost her. "We're a good balance, then, you think?"

She nodded, her curls gleaming burnished copper in the candlelight. He hoped that they would have a little girl with curls like that. It was bred into him, to want children, to give them his name, but Leigh's decisions would be honored—but then…. Jarek rubbed his chin. Considering her, there would be other matters in which he would win. Some for her, some for him—it was good. He loved her for her softness, but also for her strength.

"I promise that if anything like this happens again, I will consider what you want.

"And I will consider that you are predictable. That in cer-

tain situations, you will react the same." Then, because his
doubts and emotions had stirred him enough, he asked, "Shall
we eat?"

She frowned at him. "You just switched from something
very important to the mundane. And you're grinning when
before you were fierce and angry. Let's keep to the program,
dearest."

He loved the endearment, treasured and wallowed in it. He
couldn't resist teasing her. "You brought me dinner, it is here
and getting cold. A woman should provide food for a man.
That is the program."

Leigh picked up a bread roll and threw it at him. He caught
it and tore off a chunk, chewing it as he tried not to grin.

"I'm not going to brood about this, you know. You think
I'll never do anything really impetuous, don't you? You're
very certain of me. Good old Leigh. Dependable Leigh. Unex-
citing Leigh. Maybe I don't like that. I can manage off a
schedule, you know."

"Show me." He loved to challenge her, to watch those gold
eyes flash.

"All right. We're having dinner tomorrow night with Morris, and I want to give you something to remember—just for
you."

Moments later, Jarek sat very still, his body hardened.
Dressed only in the Stepanov necklace, Leigh was calmly eating her food and chatting away about the customers at the
shop.

He couldn't talk. He couldn't think. He stared at the bare
smooth skin in front of him and placed the glass he'd been
holding aside. If he hadn't, the wine might have spilled—or
he might have crushed the glass, lost in his desire for her.
When her toes rubbed his inner thigh, his hand shackled her
ankle. The candlelight flickered over her sultry, knowing expression, glittered on the necklace and caressed her breasts.
Jarek's voice came out raw and low and uneven. "So this is

what I'm supposed to think about while you're chatting with Morris?''

Her smile was impish. ''I'm good, aren't I? I think I might be really good.''

Jarek tried not to drool as she stretched luxuriously, then her expression changed to serious. She spoke quietly. ''I need to tell you that I may do something you don't approve of— but I'm going to do it. It's something I think that needs to be done, a very personal matter of a closure.''

The contrast between sensuality and the warning stunned him. Would she go to Lars and—? ''Tell me.''

''Oh, you'll know soon enough. It's something I need to do as a woman, something very personal. But what you have to remember, other than this, is that I love you. And don't worry, I'm not attempting to settle with Lars or anyone like him by myself.''

''Come here,'' he whispered rawly, his pulses humming and hot as Leigh stood slowly, very properly folded her napkin and fluffed her hair, and then came to sit on his lap.

Jarek held the moment inside him, treasuring the pleasure of Leigh snuggling close and fragrant against him…as if she were coming home to stay in his arms. She smoothed his hair and kissed his lids.

His body went stark rigid as she whispered into his ear, breathing huskily. ''My parents think they'll stay here through the winter. They are really happy. Ryan wants his own place, but he's staying, too. Fadey and he are in some massive plan to build Stepanov surfboards, and Ryan is going to market and demonstrate them. And he likes working with furniture. I would never have thought to bring them here. But because of you, I think my family can be happy in one place—together. And I can watch Ed's and Bliss's health problems much better. Bliss thinks she's going to help out at the small town clinic. She does have a way of calming and soothing people in distress.''

Jarek caressed her breasts, loving how the tips etched his palm, how she breathed when he touched her, how she smelled—that feminine scent that was so arousing. "You're covering your bases for tomorrow night, aren't you? Making certain that everything goes smoothly with Morris?"

"It would help if you were well behaved. Morris is my friend and I want him to think the best of you. You can save the irritating, arrogant, macho stuff for me, because now I'm learning how to serve it back to you." Leigh inhaled sharply, her fingers digging into his shoulder as he caressed her intimately. "But I'm not expecting perfect behavior just now—"

Jarek stood with her in his arms and carried her to his bed. Lying and watching him, her body curved and pale, the necklace glittering at her throat, she was all that he wanted, or would want.

"Thank you," Leigh whispered against his throat as they danced the next night. Dressed in a suit and tie, Jarek was gorgeous. But she knew that hard body beneath the clothes, how much he would demand and how much she would give. She knew *that* look, the desire packed into it, even though he spoke quietly with Mikhail and Morris. There was that slight trembling of his rough calloused hands, the reverence with which he touched her. But then, she had demanded and had taken her share, too.

The impact of the Stepanov brothers, dressed to kill in the formal dining room had sent shock waves through the other women. Equally tall, magnetic, a contrast of civilization and primitive sexuality, the brothers were breathtaking. An easy smile, a nod of their heads and women sighed. Clearly both were out to charm, and Mikhail treated her more like a sister than a business acquaintance.

With the experience of an older brother who sometimes liked to nettle a younger one, Mikhail had been very attentive and had asked to dance with her. The small band played songs from the big band era. Mikhail moved smoothly, nodding and smiling with professional ease at the guests. He didn't seem at all like the man who had worked in the shop, a sweaty bandanna tied around his forehead and periodically yelling "Hey!" to the vibrant Russian folk music. Or the man raging about Ellie Lathrop's latest demand, the "damned nursery idea."

"You're wearing the necklace. Next you'll be wearing the Stepanov name. My brother won't want to wait. Don't think that will help you put that display rack outside of the shop doorway," Mikhail murmured with a grin.

Jarek had only placed the offer on the table, and it was for her to decide.

She still had one problem to resolve, a conclusion to Annabelle's hold over Jarek. She needed to prove to herself that Annabelle was truly gone. "Mikhail, you know that display rack would be good merchandising. You're just enjoying sparring with me."

"Of course," he'd said in that familiar way. "But you rise to the challenge so nicely. My brother wasn't likely to choose a weak woman to love. Not now. He needs that edge, that excitement you give him."

"I do?" She hadn't thought of herself as an exciting woman. But then she remembered Jarek's expression as she undressed for dinner last night.

Mikhail had sighed dramatically. "Is it always left to the older brother to explain everything? Jarek is fascinated by you. He's in love with you, of course."

She couldn't help returning Mikhail's knowing smile. "Of course. How could he not be?"

Mikhail's unexpected burst of laughter had drawn looks, but filled with happiness, Leigh hadn't cared.

Tonight, during the business dinner, she was aware of Jarek's every move, the sensual way he stroked an icy glass rim, the way he inclined his head, listening intently. When she could not see him, she could feel him.

Jarek had watched her across the dance floor, smiling up at Mikhail, then he'd moved toward her. She could read the way Jarek's body relaxed slightly, gracefully, as he slowly walked toward her with almost an animal sensuality. In response, electricity streaked beneath her skin, and low in her stomach, the nudge of sensual heat began.

Mikhail had smiled blandly when Jarek had cut in, whisking her away. "That's enough of that," he'd stated grimly.

Leigh's body relaxed against Jarek's, the feeling of coming home as his arms tightened around her. "Dinner was perfect. And so were you."

"Did you doubt it?" Jarek looked over Leigh's curls to the man studying them on the dance floor. His hand on her back tightened as he met Morris's look. "I want to pick you up and carry you out of here."

She smiled against his throat. Jarek made her feel like a woman—feminine, desired, pampered, thoroughly loved. Black and tight, very proper in the front and sinfully low in the back, the dress emphasized Leigh's curves and had just the effect on Jarek that she wanted. She wore the necklace and no other jewelry to distract from it.

As those dark green eyes slowly traveled down her body and up to her face—she knew that Jarek desired her, that he was remembering how they had made love several times during the night. The impact was enough to weaken her knees and start her senses humming. She saw him over her, arms braced, his possessive hungry expression, and she carried with her the sensual lodging of his desire within her throughout the day. She had no doubt that he intended she remember, too. Each touch had been a claiming, a temptation for her to answer and take.

Marcella came to smile seductively at Jarek as she tapped Leigh on the shoulder. "May I cut in?"

Jarek scowled at her. "No. Go away. I am engaged."

Marcella seemed so crestfallen that Leigh almost felt sorry for her. The woman seemed to slink away.

"You're going to be with him tonight, aren't you?"

"First, let's clarify that we are not officially engaged, Jarek."

He shrugged as if dismissing a minor point, but that heavy-lidded sensuality said that he knew she was his. With his hand caressing her bare back, the tiny sparks shooting through her body, Leigh decided not to debate who belonged to whom. She smoothed the hair at his temples as they swayed to the music. "We have business later tonight and again early in the morning. Morris is on a short time frame. I won't—I won't be able to come to you tonight."

The lock of Jarek's jaw said he wasn't happy. "Does Morris have anything to do with the warning you served me?"

"Nothing at all. It's a woman-thing. And it's private."

"I don't think I'll like it."

"I need to handle this by myself, my love. Let me."

His rough growling noise said he didn't like the idea, but he would stand by her decision.

Two hours later as Morris sat in her suite, going over her research and reports, he shook his head and placed work aside. "It's happened, hasn't it? Love?"

Leigh turned from her desk. She loved this man, too, but in a different way. "Yes, I love him."

Morris lifted his wineglass and sipped deeply. His eyes were sad as he considered her. "It's all in the body language. His toward you, and yours toward him. He's been the problem, the reason I sensed that you were distracted, isn't he?"

When she nodded, Morris rose and stared out at the panoramic view of the ocean at night. He looked so alone that she came to stand beside him. Morris shook his head. "I thought that one day, we might—"

"Might still be friends, even as our lives changed?" she asked, wanting to ease him. "We'll always be friends."

"It's too fast, Leigh. This thing between you and Stepanov has moved like wildfire. You've never been one to take chances. I don't understand. You've always had this plan, step by step. I thought when you weren't so driven, maybe you'd see that you meant more to me than a sharp mind and good business."

Morris turned to her. "Is business the only relationship we've had?"

"No, we've had much more…trust and companionship and respect. We're friends, Morris. And good friends are difficult to find."

"I don't trust him. He's arrogant, and he's moved too fast on you. You're very vulnerable, especially after that issue with Kevin. You're used to traveling. I've watched you teethe on business and you love it, thrive on it. You won't be happy. You'll be wasting your talent."

She hadn't expected the bitterness in his voice. He'd always been so calm and understanding. "I'm going to marry Jarek, Morris. We have some issues to resolve, but the love is there, and the commitment. And I want us to remain friends."

"'Friends?'" he echoed hollowly. Then he moved suddenly, walking stiffly toward the door. "I'll see you in the morning."

"Morris—" But the door closed and Leigh was left with the emptiness of losing a long-term friend and mentor.

She leaned against the window frame and looked out at the ocean. Morris was right, the time-frame was logically too short to fall in love—but she had. Jarek was the other part of her; he gave her solace and comfort and understanding. He gave her friendship, which she'd never had. They were a good mix, a strong one, bound by love.

Moonlight caught Deadman's Rock, boldly outlining it in

the night, and she could almost hear Annabelle's soulful call to Jarek.

Leigh closed her eyes, needing his arms around her, needing his strength. In the morning, she hoped Morris would see reason…and then she would deal with Annabelle's ghost and Kamakani's legendary curse.

Then she looked at the man standing below her suite, his white dress shirt open and flowing in the wind as he stared up at her. The impact was there, hot and wild, traveling through the night. Jarek was coming for her and nothing could keep him away.

She walked out to the patio, just in time to see him lift a rope with an anchor attached to the end of it. He motioned for her to step aside and started swinging the small anchor.

The anchor hit and locked on to the sturdy railing four floors above him. Jarek tested it with his weight.

"Don't you dare—" But Jarek was already climbing up, and Leigh's heart stopped as she watched. She motioned frantically for him to stop, to lower himself to safety.

Mikhail, his hands on his hips, had come to stand below Jarek. "The railing is sturdy enough. But he might not be, once I get my hands on him," Mikhail called quietly.

A woman screamed on the floor below as Jarek climbed upward. "A little problem with the elevator," he stated calmly to her. "Lovely night, isn't it? Ah, I don't suppose you have any flowers, do you? I forgot mine. Lovely peignoir, by the way."

"You're that Stepanov man, the one in the dining room tonight, aren't you? Here, wait—oh, how romantic. You're going to see her, aren't you? The one you held so romantically tonight? As if you cherished her more than anything, consumed by passion for her, would do anything for her, would want to hold and love her all the days of your life?"

"Without her, I am nothing," Jarek stated dramatically and placed his free hand over his heart.

"Ohh! How lovely! I'll be just a minute."

Leigh watched, horrified, as Jarek reached out a hand to claim a bouquet, which he tucked into his waistband. He leaned toward the woman, who placed a single stem in his teeth. He climbed upward, a full rose bobbing at the end of the stem.

"I'll kill him," Leigh muttered as her fingers ached from gripping the rope, fearing that it would loosen from the anchor and drop him to the ground.

"You're so lucky, honey," the woman called upward to Leigh. "Goodness, he's so romantic. Yoo-hoo, Mr. Stepanov on the ground there. If this is an act for the benefit of the guests, it's delightful. I'll tell my friends about it."

"I assure you, this event has not occurred before. Possibilities for a repeat performance are not likely," Mikhail stated formally and stepped away into the darkness.

When Jarek climbed over the railing, Leigh threw a glass of ice water at him. He was sheer reaction to the fear and anger shaking her. Now she knew how Jarek felt when he saw Lars grabbing her, a sickening fear, though her anger couldn't have possibly matched his. "Don't ever, ever do that again."

Jarek swiped away the water dripping from his face and released the rose to a patio table. "Did you think I wouldn't come for you? Did you think I would lie on my empty bed and think of you, just after the night we pledged our love?"

She took the bouquet he solemnly handed her. "Thank you. But there are halls and elevators."

His head tilted just that bit. "I didn't want to meet Morris. When I saw you alone at the window, I knew he had gone."

Leigh nuzzled the fragrant blossoms. He was here and safe and nothing else mattered. "If you were thinking about me, a telephone call would have done."

He shook his head. "It's not the same thing. I couldn't smell you, watch you, touch you, feel you."

She couldn't help smiling—simply smiling with the pleasure he brought her, the warmth enclosing her heart. Jarek bent to pick her up, arms around her hips, nuzzling her breasts as he walked into her bedroom and kicked the door closed behind them.

In the morning, he was gone, the single rose resting on his pillow. A plain wedding band circled the stem—Jarek's statement that he wanted marriage and soon.

She smiled dreamily, imagining the combination of the traditional Stepanovs' wedding ideas—Mary Jo would want to plan an elaborate wedding, one she never had with Fadey. She'd want an engagement party and all the festivities. From a wealthy Texan family, Mary Jo knew exactly how to throw "a do."

On the other hand, Ed and Bliss would prefer a less stressful route.

Leigh made a mental note to start carrying her worry stone. Jarek could be stubborn and he might not want to wait. In contrast to Fadey's and Jarek's outright opinions, Mary Jo's cool determination was powerful in the long run.

The sealed envelope slid beneath her door was from Morris. "I understand. I'll work this out and we'll be friends. But for now, I'm leaving. I saw last night how very special he is to you, and you were radiant with him. As your mother would say, your aura was perfectly blooming. That's very special. I wouldn't wish you anything but just exactly that. We'll work out business arrangements to your satisfaction. He's not the kind of man to want you away from him. I don't blame him. Your friend, Morris."

Leigh held the note close to her chest and ached for the man who had obviously waited for her. "Oh, Morris. I hope you find what you want."

At six o'clock in the morning, Deadman's Rock loomed, hidden by fog.

Annabelle waited out there and Leigh was determined to tear her away from Jarek.

"I am too selfish to share Jarek with a ghost, or with his guilt," Leigh whispered, and then called Ryan.

Jarek stood on the shoreline, watching the sun skim across the water. At four o'clock in the afternoon, Leigh wasn't at the shop. Mikhail had said she closed it at noon and Morris had checked out earlier. It was now six o'clock.

Had she decided to go to Morris after all?

That thought chilled Jarek. He watched the vacationers' boats glide past on the swells, and he shook his head. She loved him—not with reserve, but wide-open. It was there in her eyes, in her touch.

Where was she?

He refused to call her parents, to check up on her. He trusted her, but *where was she*?

Ryan was uneasy, too. He wasn't talking and avoided looking at Jarek.

Sensing his son's distraction, Fadey had placed an arm around Jarek and had cautioned him. "Love her, but give her the time she needs alone. It's a woman-thing. You will have to learn to give her privacy in these matters—the things a woman decides within herself. Like when your mother first knew she carried you...she wanted to hold that secret inside her, just that bit, to think and turn it, much as a man would study a good piece of wood, trying to see what it held. I had to wait—though I knew by the signs—for her to tell me, because that was how she wanted it to be. A man does not always understand, to him it seems so easy. But a woman—you will learn—give her time to herself to settle what is important to her."

Seagulls swooped across the cerulean sky, the frothing tide caressing the shore and scent of fear carried on the saltwater breeze.

Where was Leigh?

His mother knew, but like Ryan, she wasn't talking. "She

was here, and I understand,'' Mary Jo had said quietly. ''She's doing what she must. Let her.''

Unable to stay inside, Jarek walked along the shore. He noted a sleek expensive boat, white sails lowered, motoring into the tourists' docking. A mother with children called to them, urging them to collect the shells and driftwood in their sand pails. She folded her chair, and began packing away the clutter. Obviously lost in her thoughts, she tossed bread to the sand and watched the gulls devour it.

Why would Leigh need time alone?

Jarek skimmed the tourists and the piers, hoping to catch sight of her. He'd leave her alone—he just wanted to know that she was safe.

He smiled whimsically, mocking himself. Or could he leave her alone?

From a distant point where the bluish-gray water merged into the bright sky near Deadman's Rock, a small motorboat prowled toward Amoteh. It was only a dot at first, and Jarek watched without interest, his mind focused on Leigh.

The boat came closer, the sound of the motor humming as it continued directly toward him. Tourists, he thought, without enough sense to—he studied the figure in the boat, and decided it was probably a boy coming back from fishing.

Then a slender white arm shot high to wave and the burnished red of Leigh's curls caught the sunlight. He ran toward where the swells were carrying the boat to shore, then waded in to tug the rope, hauling the boat safely to the wet sand.

He couldn't speak, glancing at Deadman's Rock, and understanding immediately that her course had come straight from the passage where Annabelle had died. He pivoted back to Leigh, who had raised the outboard motor with surprising expertise.

''What do you think you are doing?'' he demanded as together they hauled the boat high on the sand.

Then he knew from Leigh's expression—she'd gone to

Strawberry Hill on the same course as Annabelle. A nightmare passed through him, leaving his heart icy. Was Leigh also fascinated with the Hawaiian chieftain's legend?

Because he hurt and he feared, Jarek turned to walk away. She called out to him, but he kept walking. In the distance he saw Ryan, lowering binoculars, Ed and Bliss standing next to him. He saw Mikhail outlined on the steps near Amoteh and ignored Leigh's second call.

He heard her running behind him, and still he didn't turn, wrapped in his fear that something might have happened to her.

He heard a pounding sound, or was it fear still tearing through his heart?

Then the impact of Leigh's body hit him in the back, her arms looping around this throat. He staggered and righted, and Leigh held firm, edging higher to wrap her legs around him. Automatically his arms went behind him to support her bottom as if she were a child.

But she wasn't a child, she was the woman he loved and she'd just done something inexplicable, terrifying him. He kept walking, partly from anger, and more from fear.

She panted close to his ear. "I had to run and jump off that driftwood log back there, but I've bagged you. You're mine and you're not getting away."

"Why? Why would you do such a thing?" He didn't know whether to charge into an argument or kiss her. For now, trudging along the shore with her clinging to him safely was enough.

She kissed his cheek and set her chin on his shoulder. "Because I wanted you to know that I'll always come back. I'm not Annabelle, Jarek. I'm me, and I'm safe."

"You might not have been. There are currents—"

"Ryan told me about them. You think I could have a brother who lived on a surfboard for most of his young life and wouldn't know something about how to rescue him?

You're too arrogant by far, sweetheart, if you think I can't manage a motorboat across a good stretch of water on a clear day."

"You were lucky," he grumbled as she playfully nuzzled his throat.

"I'm good, my husband-to-be. Really good. And I love you, and only you. I'm too selfish to want to share you. I came back, and that's what's important."

He smiled at that, eased by her label for him. "Don't do it again."

"Of course not, not without you. But this one time was important. For us and for me. I wanted to put Annabelle in the past, where she belongs."

Jarek shook his head and lowered her to the ground. He tugged her to him, and brushed back her windswept curls. This was the woman who held his heart—all of it without guilt caused by another woman. He'd remember Annabelle, but everything that he was or would be was in his arms, loving him—of course, he loved her more.

Leigh looked up at him with those gold eyes, her expression soft with love. "Remember that I came back, Jarek. Let's start from here, shall we?"

After the September traditional wedding that Jarek insisted they have, the family gathered in the Stepanov home.

Fadey sat back in his favorite chair and watched his new daughter serve traditional Russian tea. She was beautiful, of course, beaming and happy, enveloped by love for Jarek, just as it should be. The bridal gown was to his liking, not so modern, but a dress like a woman should wear on her wedding day—one to dance in. The flower coronet over Leigh's bright curls reminded him of the old country, and how Mary Jo had looked in their own wedding.

It was good, he thought as his new daughter served the *zavarka* in the *chaepitie* ceremony as he had taught her. The

samovar he had ordered for her was only electric, not so good
as the old kind, but he knew Leigh would treasure it. And the
tea service every bride should have.

Fadey sighed with pleasure and sipped his tea. If only Mikhail—but he tossed that thought away. His son had been badly
hurt, his unborn child aborted, his wife running off to be a
wild woman. But Mikhail was only waiting, just as Jarek had
waited. The woman would come; Fadey could feel it.

For now, there was Jarek, that sadness gone, his heart too
filled with love for anything else. Fadey knew that look, it had
been—and still was his own. He knew the happiness that
waited for Jarek.

Mary Jo brushed a tear from Fadey's cheek. "Now, darlin'.
It's all right."

"I'm just so happy," Fadey stated unevenly. "My heart is
so full."

The shout came from someone unexpected. Bliss stood and
whirled around, catching her daughter's hand and twirling her.
"Hey!"

Ed stood up and took Jarek's hand. "Hey!"

"Oh," Mary Jo said warily as she collected Fadey's teacup.
"I'd better start moving everything breakable out of the room.
Fadey—roll up the rugs and start the music."

Months later, Jarek looked down at Leigh making her way
to him. He stood in the doorway of their unfinished house, his
father's saw ripping through the morning and Mikhail's and
Ryan's and Ed's hammers banging in rhythm to a furious Russian folk song.

The November wind lifted Leigh's coppery hair, longer now
and rich with sunlight. The wind pasted her clothes to her
body, curves that would change soon because their child nestled within her. He'd found many times during their marriage
that it was best to let Leigh choose her own time—and now
she had.

As if he couldn't tell by the way she glowed, by the quiet introspective way she looked at the small room, as yet unfinished. He'd purposely slowed finishing it, because he'd secretly hoped—

His wife stood beneath him now, beaming up at him, her hands on her hips. "I'm pregnant, of course," she yelled against the wind and the music and the saw and hammers.

"We know, dear," Bliss called from an open window. "How wonderful!"

"I am going to be a grandma at last," Mary Jo breathed as if relieved.

"Of course," Jarek yelled back as he hurried down to kiss the woman he loved.

* * * * *

Don't miss Mikhail Stepanov's story,
told in the second book in Cait London's
sensual new miniseries,

Heartbreakers,

which features to-die-for heroes
and the women they come to love.

On sale February 2003 from Silhouette Desire.

presents

A brand-new miniseries about the Connellys of Chicago,
a wealthy, powerful American family tied by blood to the
royal family of the island kingdom of Altaria.
They're wealthy, powerful and rocked by
scandal, betrayal…and passion!

Look for a whole year of glamorous and
utterly romantic tales in 2002:

January: **TALL, DARK & ROYAL** by Leanne Banks

February: **MATERNALLY YOURS** by Kathie DeNosky

March: **THE SHEIKH TAKES A BRIDE** by Caroline Cross

April: **THE SEAL'S SURRENDER** by Maureen Child

May: **PLAIN JANE & DOCTOR DAD** by Kate Little

June: **AND THE WINNER GETS…MARRIED!** by Metsy Hingle

July: **THE ROYAL & THE RUNAWAY BRIDE** by Kathryn Jensen

August: **HIS E-MAIL ORDER WIFE** by Kristi Gold

September: **THE SECRET BABY BOND** by Cindy Gerard

October: **CINDERELLA'S CONVENIENT HUSBAND**
by Katherine Garbera

November: **EXPECTING…AND IN DANGER** by Eileen Wilks

December: **CHEROKEE MARRIAGE DARE**
by Sheri WhiteFeather

Where love comes alive™

eHARLEQUIN.com

community | membership

buy books | authors | online reads | magazine | learn to write

buy books

Your one-stop shop for great reads at great prices. We have all your favorite Harlequin, Silhouette, MIRA and Steeple Hill books, as well as a host of other bestsellers in Other Romances. Discover a wide array of new releases, bargains and hard-to find books today!

learn to write

Become the writer you always knew you could be: get tips and tools on how to craft the perfect romance novel and have your work critiqued by professional experts in romance fiction. Follow your dream now!

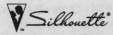

Silhouette®

Where love comes alive™—online...

Visit us at
www.eHarlequin.com

You are invited to enter the exclusive, masculine world of the...

TEXAS Cattleman's Club
The Last Bachelor

Silhouette Desire's powerful miniseries features five wealthy Texas bachelors—all members of the state's most prestigious club— who set out to uncover a traitor in their midst... and discover their true loves!

THE MILLIONAIRE'S PREGNANT BRIDE
by Dixie Browning
February 2002 (SD #1420)

HER LONE STAR PROTECTOR
by Peggy Moreland
March 2002 (SD #1426)

TALL, DARK...AND FRAMED?
by Cathleen Galitz
April 2002 (SD #1433)

THE PLAYBOY MEETS HIS MATCH
by Sara Orwig
May 2002 (SD #1438)

THE BACHELOR TAKES A WIFE
by Jackie Merritt
June 2002 (SD #1444)

Available at your favorite retail outlet.

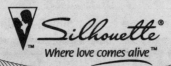

Silhouette®
Where love comes alive™

If you enjoyed what you just read,
then we've got an offer you can't resist!

Take 2 bestselling
love stories FREE!
Plus get a FREE surprise gift!

Clip this page and mail it to Silhouette Reader Service™

IN U.S.A.	**IN CANADA**
3010 Walden Ave.	P.O. Box 609
P.O. Box 1867	Fort Erie, Ontario
Buffalo, N.Y. 14240-1867	L2A 5X3

YES! Please send me 2 free Silhouette Desire® novels and my free surprise gift. After receiving them, if I don't wish to receive anymore, I can return the shipping statement marked cancel. If I don't cancel, I will receive 6 brand-new novels every month, before they're available in stores! In the U.S.A., bill me at the bargain price of $3.34 plus 25¢ shipping and handling per book and applicable sales tax, if any*. In Canada, bill me at the bargain price of $3.74 plus 25¢ shipping and handling per book and applicable taxes**. That's the complete price and a savings of at least 10% off the cover prices—what a great deal! I understand that accepting the 2 free books and gift places me under no obligation ever to buy any books. I can always return a shipment and cancel at any time. Even if I never buy another book from Silhouette, the 2 free books and gift are mine to keep forever.

225 SEN DFNS
326 SEN DFNT

Name _____ (PLEASE PRINT) _____

Address _____ Apt.# _____

City _____ State/Prov. _____ Zip/Postal Code _____

* Terms and prices subject to change without notice. Sales tax applicable in N.Y.
** Canadian residents will be charged applicable provincial taxes and GST.
   All orders subject to approval. Offer limited to one per household and not valid to
   current Silhouette Desire® subscribers.
   ® are registered trademarks of Harlequin Enterprises Limited.

DES01   ©1998 Harlequin Enterprises Limited